"GENIALITY"

(The Equilibrist series: Vol. 2)

Erasmus Cromwell-Smith II

ECS

ERASMUS CROMWELL-SMITH

Geniality

®Erasmus Cromwell-Smith II.

®Erasmus Press.

ISBN: 978-1-7369968-0-5

Library of Congress Number: 1-10411604161

Publisher: Erasmus Press.

Editor: Elisa Arraiz Lucca

Cover and Interior Design: Alfredo Sainz Blanco.

Proofreading: María Elena Peña, D. Suster, Tracy-Ann Wynter

Second edition. Printed in USA.

erasmuscromwellsmith.com

Erasmus Cromwell-Smith Books

In English	**En Español**
The Equilibrist series	La serie El equilibrista
(Inspirational/Philosophical)	Inspiracional/Filosófica)
The Happiness Triangle (Vol. 1)	El triángulo de la Felicidad (V. 1)
Geniality (Vol. 2)	Genialidad (Vol. 2)
The Magic in Life (Vol. 3)	La magia de la vida (Vol. 3)
Poetry in Equilibrium (Vol. 4)	Poesía en equilibrio (Vol. 4)

(Young Adults)	**Jóvenes Adultos**
The Orloj of Prague (Vol. 5)	El Orloj de Praga (Vol. 5)
The Orloj of Venice (Vol. 6)	El Orloj de Venecia (Vol. 6)
The Orloj of Paris (Vol. 7)	El Orloj de Paris (Vol. 7)
The Orloj of Munich (Vol. 8)	El Orloj de Munich (Vol. 8)
Poetry in Balance (Vol. 9)	Poesía en Balance (Vol. 9)

The South Beach Conversational Method (Educational)
• Spanish
• German
• French
• Italian
• Portuguese

El Método Conversacional South Beach (Educacional)
• Inglés,
• Alemán
• Francés
• Italiano
• Portugués

The Nicolas Tosh Series   (Sci-fi)
Algoritm-323 (Vol. 1)
Tosh (Vol. 2)

As Nelson Hamel*
The Paradise Island Series
(Action/Thriller)
Miami Beach, Dangerous Lifestyles (Vol. 1)
The Rb Hackers Series (Sci/fi)
The Rebel Hackers of Point Breeze (Vol.1

* In collaboration with Charles Sibley.
All books are or will be included in Audiobook

For my children,
"Our blue unicorns in life only exist
   if we can see them"

Table of Contents

Note by the author,

My father, Erasmus Cromwell-Smith, was born in the Welsh Hamlet of Hay-on-Wye, also known as "Booktown". He grew up surrounded by books, antique bookstores, and a trio of eclectic antiquarian mentors. Eventually, the future pedagogue earned a scholarship to Oxford and then to Harvard, where in 1976 he met and fell in love with my mother, Victoria Emerson-Lloyd. They lived together for two years, and then for no apparent reason, she vanished. Alone, without the love of his live, he began a lifelong career as an occasional author, an English Literature and poetry teacher at prestigious New England educational institutions.

In 2017, after being diagnosed with terminal brain cancer, he decided to deviate from his normal teaching curriculum to narrate and reveal a number of secrets from his peculiar life story under the prism of poetry.

In his classes, my father went back in time to the years of his youth and narrated his life through a series of rich and unforgettable teaching sessions. Predictably, his health started to deteriorate until miraculously, a state-of-the-art treatment put his cancer into remission.

Then, on the last day of the 2017 academic year, as he was about to finish the semester, my mother showed up forty years after her disappearance. This story begins precisely at that moment in time – when they reunite. It was an unforgettable moment, they treasured for the rest of their lives. A few months later, with my mother now by his side, living together in a campus home, they became energized and rejuvenated. That's when my father decided to repeat the prior academic year's format by continuing to tell his life's story through the mantel of poetry.

Thus, in his 2018 class, Professor Cromwell-Smith veered off the standard curriculum again. He took his students back in time, to the mid-1970s to the moment when my mother and he met at Harvard. With his class of 2018, he delved into their courtship and eventually how they won over each other's hearts and lived together for two years.

"Geniality" is about the ultimate triumph of optimism and the sheer power of unconditional love. It is also about timeless life anecdotes and experiences within my parents' love story and their infatuated, passionate life during those two years at Harvard. It encompasses as well, the magical journey the two of them embarked on, by continuing my father's childhood tradition of befriending and getting acquainted with intriguing and eccentric antiquarians, similar to his early life back in Wales – but this time in New England. His new mentors shared with my parents several profound life lessons and wisdom which were expressed through old scribbles, essays, and poetry. I hope "Geniality" inspires you to live a full life and squeeze out the best it's got to offer. I sincerely wish you to enjoy "Geniality" as much as I did in creating it.

Erasmus Cromwell-Smith, II

CHAPTER 1

OPTIMISM

Royal Cambridge Scholastic Institute (2018)
(Erasmus and Victoria's Campus Home)

"Don't take too long my love, I am waiting for you," Victoria teases with a wink as she sends him off to class with a warm kiss and a hug. Professor Erasmus Cromwell-Smith is a new man. His sad demeanor, worn out, and unkempt appearance is all gone. He wears the look of love! The hand of a woman caring for him is obvious, especially with his impeccable, perfectly trimmed, and pressed look. On this first day of his 2018 class, he finds himself with an enthusiastic crowd and the auditorium filled to capacity.

(University's Auditorium)

"Good morning. How's everyone?"

"Awesome, Professor Cromwell," replies the highly motivated student body to the illustrious pedagogue's delight as they have all learned his favorite word.

"I simply ask that you always be on time – no excuses." He gazes intensely at everyone as he emphasizes the remark. "Alright, let us begin then."

"The love of my life, Vicky, and I have reunited after forty years, thanks in part to one of my students in last year's class." Cheers and applause interrupt the professor. He smiles and waits until it dies down.

"The enabling student turned out to be Vicky's youngest daughter and her participation in my class was completely fortuitous as was her realization of who I was. Allow me to explain. Last year at this time, I had been diagnosed with terminal brain cancer, which thanks to a revolutionary treatment is in remission at present." Again, the entire class stands up to clap and cheer in joy. Cromwell-Smith obliges with a smile and a slight nod, but after a while feeling uncomfortable, the professor interrupts the unruly crowd.

"Last year, assuming I didn't have much time left, I decided to change the format of the class into an evocative reminiscence of my life through the prism of poetry. Then as I moved along, after a number of class sessions, Vicky's daughter figured out who I was and decided to tell her mom that she had found me."

"Is the student your real daughter Professor?" asks a student from the audience. The professor pauses, hand on his chin with a kind of startled expression, and states, "Let me explain please." He then continues without answering the question - at least not at first.

"Even though we were madly in love and had been living together for two years, Vicky's parents had other ideas in mind and separated us. One day, she simply vanished from campus. I went to her hometown in Southern Illinois and found an empty house. I never heard from her again and I never learned why either. Those were the 1970's in a small conservative midwestern town. Her parents had simply made up their minds and married her off to someone else. Then she went on to have three children with him. Years later, he got sick with cancer and passed away two years ago. Once this happened and knowing their mother's feelings, her three kids set out to find me. Then, the youngest of the three siblings ran into me quite by accident while taking my course." The professor pauses and gazing at the audience realizes that he has their full attention.

"Class, throughout the years of solitude, even within the turmoil of recent unforeseen events, in spite of the ups and downs, or the never-ending uncertainties and anxieties, I never lost my optimism towards life. Hence, with this in mind, we are now going to start this year's journey. The story you are about to hear, is about the ultimate and inexorable triumph of optimism, in spite of the unexpected bends in the road of life. We begin today with an overture of our academic journey. Please allow me to read to you an ode to the power of optimism."

"Optimism"

Optimism is a deliberate attitude
where we chose to contemplate life and its people,
through their best lights, colors, and mantels.
It is a predisposition to look, search and find,

the better angle and perspective,

on everything and everyone.

It is a natural inclination to visualize,

what is the best,

a person or circumstance has to offer.

It is that refreshing enthusiasm we bring into

all and every one of life's occurrences,

any and each of its moments.

It is that unquenchable certainty,

that there always is,

a shinier side and a brighter spot to be found.

It is that steadfast and indomitable self-confidence,

that there is always,

a better outcome possible,

in-store,

waiting for us.

Optimism is also,

that gentle, benign, and immutable self-belief,

that, there is goodness on the other side of evil,

that, there is strength in the other face of weakness,

that, there is virtue behind every flaw,

that, there is opportunity

when apparently there is none,

that, there is incandescence in obscurity

and luminescence in darkness.

Those possessed with optimism
live in another world, live an alternate life,
and contemplate it all
with a permanent twinkle in their eyes.
Optimists are always
cheerful, self-motivated, fiercely determined
and seemingly possessed with a secret elixir
that allows them to erase and wipe out,
pessimism, prejudice, negativism, and grudges,
from their lives.
Optimism always obliterates,
"the loser before the start" syndrome, from all of us.
With optimism, we see past or right through
everything and everyone.
Civilization has been built out of optimism,
progress is driven by optimism,
every single human invention, creation,
or advancement,
has taken place through
the candor, the innocence,
and the ingenuity of optimists.
And not a single transcendental milestone
in the human race,
will ever be reached, done or achieved,
without the unstoppable drive of optimism.

True, legitimate, and genuine optimism

always marches forward,

cannot be deterred, deviated, or turned back.

Optimism is utterly oblivious

to criticism, rejection, doubt or skepticism.

Authentic optimism is also malleable,

that is why,

the tougher the goals, obstacles, or challenges,

the bigger genuine optimism becomes.

Those bitten by the bug of optimism,

have "good blinders on,"

as they are immune to the contrarians

and naysayers.

In their own way

optimists intentionally "distort reality,"

until "the alternate version" of it,

becomes the new reality.

Then they enhance whatever there is available to us,

through a perennially benevolent and candid vision,

of what, may, could, would, might, and inexorably,

under such state and condition,

will be.

As Professor Cromwell-Smith completes the reading of the
scribble, optimism is in the air. His stare is profound, his smile

is serene and his body language is engaging as he pauses and allows stillness to spread through the class. Just for a few seconds, which seem like an eternity, absolute silence engulfs the auditorium and he lets optimism lie and "sink in" before he continues.

"Optimism is a deliberate attitude that, if we're not born with it, or if it's not our natural inclination, then, we must learn or teach ourselves to embrace, practice, and carve it into our spirits as if it was second nature to our persona. The gift of life is the driving force of optimism. Always remember this, optimism is the key to opening many of life's doors, those that only an optimist can see, the kind of places and outcomes only an optimist can reach, experience and enjoy. Optimism, more often than not, contains the only winning hand in the game of life," states the professor to the full attention of his class. Smiling and ready to wrap up the introductory part of the course, he brings the class back full circle.

"Today's session began a few months ago when we'd just finished the last class of the 2017 academic year. Just as we were about to leave the classroom, as her daughter found me, the love of my life, Vicky, showed up unannounced and called my name from the stands. It all reignited with my response."

Royal Cambridge Scholastic Institute (2017)

(University's Auditorium)

Last Class of the Previous Academic Year

As he wraps up his 2017 class, Professor Cromwell-Smith is elated, but emotionally spent as if just having crossed the finish line of a long race where all of the competitors were different shades of himself. He knows he is done as he has run out of words.

"Thank you all," he says with a big broad smile denoting profound gratitude. He bows his head in respect and has nothing else to add - but life does.

Then, as the final three words echo dies, the entire student body stands up to applaud and cheer. That is when he sees her in the crowd. A young girl with curly blonde hair with her hand raised, jumping up and down, trying to draw his attention.

"One moment please," he yells interrupting the crowd.

"How can I help you, young lady?" Abruptly, like there is no tomorrow, she starts to talk.

"Professor Cromwell, I first came to one of your classes last year as you were reading a wonderful Pablo Neruda poem. At that moment, I promised myself that I was going to attend your entire course this year and it turned out to be one of the most transcendental decisions I've made in my life. I didn't know then, none of us knew, that you were going to veer off curriculum and share with us your life through poetry. Then, from the very first class, a picture began to emerge, and way before you fell in love in your life story, I knew."

"Professor, my mom has never stopped loving you. That's why I didn't have the fortitude to come to one of your classes as I assumed correctly that it was going to be about the breakup. Her parents simply didn't want her to marry you, but rather someone they had chosen since her childhood. That's how she married my father and had three children of whom I am the youngest. Then, when my father died last summer, after five years of an agonizing illness, all three of us decided to find the man she so adores, reveres, and worships – you! God works in mysterious ways professor as it didn't take us long to find you and in my case to get to know you and feel firsthand my mother's other half - her only true love in life."

Professor Cromwell's knot in his throat renders him unable to speak or breathe for a moment; then, when he gathers the strength to speak, another unexpected bend in the road awaits him.

The voice from the past comes from the very top of the stands. "Erasmus!"

He then sees her for the very first time in 40 something years. The familiar tone of voice he hears has a touch of hesitation, perhaps anguish. It is deeply emotional even primal and at the same time, it sounds like a lament and a plea, both on the verge of succumbing to pure joy-saturated love - coming straight from the longing heart of his other half.

"I am right here," she proclaims. "I am right here my love," she affirms, as time comes to a standstill and true love graces them once more.

"Victoria!" exclaims Professor Erasmus Cromwell-Smith, his lower lip trembling.

Right then, he explodes and takes off running uncontrollably up the auditorium stairs.

"Victoria," he mumbles, this time with a broken voice overcome by emotion as he climbs two steps at a time.

At first, Vicky is paralyzed and in shock when she sees Erasmus running towards her and hears him calling her name for the first time in four decades. She starts running down the stairs as well until literally crashing into him. With both his arms holding her tightly, in an instant, Erasmus becomes once more the safe and protective harbor she has longed for her entire life, one where she never feels unprotected, sad, or alone. Next, in an impetuous moment, they totally lose control in front of the entire class.

The auditorium grows completely quiet and in complicity, as every single soul in attendance is transfixed by the reality of furious unstoppable love, making itself present; as if hers and his life's story (which many of them learned through the course of their previous academic year) has just jumped out of a movie that is playing right in front of them. Staring at each other intensely, Vicky and Erasmus hold both their faces with the palms of their hands while keeping the tip of their noses impossibly close. They both are panting and gasping for air while crying and smiling a little, as bare and raw emotions pour out of them. Then, while not able to take their eyes off each other as they ignore the two hundred plus attendees, Erasmus tenderly takes Victoria's hand and they exit the auditorium walking deliberately slow. Once outside, on a glorious day and right under the moist campus forest, they start kissing all over each other's faces, in quick bursts that are frantic expressions of indomitable passion. It all becomes surreal and intensely emotional for the longing twosome. Seemingly, Erasmus and Victoria possess no time to spare and have succumbed to the power of now, squeezing every second out of it, as if there is no tomorrow.

Boston (2017)

(Downtown, Riverside Walk)

Hours later as they walk the city streets, they are already in their own world; and as they let go of the past, calmness and comfort settle in, placing the present in its proper place, allowing them to start walking into the future together.

"Vicky, your daughter changed my life today. It's not only that by bringing you, she gave me the greatest gift a man still in love can receive, but she also rendered a beautiful and inspiring homage, to the devotion and abnegation you demonstrated for your dying husband. It is not only something I will never forget but something I should memorialize as well."

Vicky gently places two fingers over his mouth and whispers. "Shhh my love, this moment is only ours and ours alone."

In a trance, Erasmus suddenly opens his worn-out leather briefcase, and on a crumpled piece of paper, furiously starts to write. Vicky knows better and simply contemplates him as she always did back then, in awe and wonder. Then, a while later when he is done, he starts to read the scribble to her with deep passion and forceful emotion, expressing exactly how much he values what she did for her dying husband.

"Small Sacrifices"

Sometimes life presents us
with seemingly impossible tasks
and insurmountable challenges, so demanding,
that we don't really know where to begin,
much less if we can respond or live up to them,
or even if we will be able
to hold on to the very end.
Sometimes life presents us with seemingly
huge sacrifices,
that more often than not,
come dressed in tragedy and pain.
Those moments test our entire self

and every task expected of us,

is tough, trying, unsavory, and even filthy,

to execute and endure.

These calls of duty

present themselves to us

as very difficult sacrifices,

ones where every inch and instinct

of our ego and selfishness,

reject and easily find excuses

to avoid or even start, anything at all.

They include the people close to us,

that cannot take care of themselves,

or are handicapped, even terminally ill

and need assistance day in and day out,

and for a while, for long or the remainder

of their lives,

they are entirely in our hands.

Then there are those,

that are deprived of their freedom,

and depend, and rely on our love, strength,

and support,

as we depend on theirs.

There are also, those that are hungry or homeless,

or those in need of guidance, mentoring, tutoring,

coaching or life lessons,

but none have anything to offer us in a way

of material things.

These are some of those moments,

when life and God,

come calling to test us on

how good we are inside.

What is our quality and worthiness

as human beings?

What is our heart really made of?

How ready are we to sacrifice and give much

without truly expecting anything in return?

In reality, these are just small sacrifices

and in a way, gifts

that are asked and required of us

in return for all of those

that we receive and have received in the past.

Sometimes life presents us

with seemingly huge sacrifices,

that are not such,

as they are opportunities

for us to pay forward,

the greatest gift of all

one already given to us in kind,

"the gift of life."

As the gentle river breeze takes Erasmus' beautiful words away, Victoria looks at him with teary eyes expressing immense gratitude. She caresses his face as if reassuring herself that he's really there.

"What's next for us?" Erasmus suddenly asks in doubt, driven by painful memories of the past quickly creeping in - about to take hold of his rational self.

She catches them on the fly and states, "Life Erasmus. That's what's ahead of us, life together, finally." Victoria takes a hold of his hand and squeezes tightly. Then, looking at him straight in the eye, she reassures Erasmus from deep within herself, "I will never leave you again my love. Never."

The infatuated twosome continue to walk, holding hands, along Main Street and then alongside the Charles River. A star-studded night serves as their "private amphitheater" ceiling. Vicky feels happy and illusioned. Erasmus, on the other hand, wants to believe with all his heart, but he's still full of doubts and fears.

Royal Cambridge Scholastic Institute (2018)
(University's Auditorium)

The bell has been ringing for a while when the class and the professor come back to the present where a fitting conclusion awaits them. "Class, that magical day when Vicky and I reunited after such a long time, is clear testimony about the unstoppable, sheer power of unconditional love and the inexorable triumph of optimism in life. For this reason, you must never, ever, let your optimism slip or wane. Keep in mind though, it is a deliberate attitude. You are a positivist because you decide to be such, because you want it; hence, you always look for the brighter, better angle, and best outcome on life and people. Next class, we will go back to my days at Harvard in the 1970s and revisit how Victoria and I fell in love. I had written about the good news to one of my childhood mentors, a beautiful and diminutive lady who was an antiquarian in my hometown in Wales. My term of endearment for her was Mrs. V. Then, she wrote back shortly thereafter and provided me with priceless wisdom and precious advice about love. But, at the end of her missive, she complained a little about the fact that I had not told her how I had won Vicky's heart. When we return to class, I will begin with what I replied back to her, as I tried to satisfy her queries. With this being said, that'll be all for today. See you all next week."

Then, as the professor leaves, some of the students react to the sights and sounds they have just witnessed.

"I wouldn't have missed this course for the world," states a second timer.

"He seems like a new man. Happy and full of energy," states another.

"There is only one way to describe it. True love found him," states an enthusiastic young lady.

"Again," finishes off another one.

And that is the last word to be heard as the students all nod their heads with expressions of hopeful expectations to find true love as well.

CHAPTER 2

OF FATE AND FAIRY TALES

Royal Cambridge Scholastic Institute (2018)
(Erasmus and Victoria's Campus Home)

"Dear, don't you ever leave my life," Victoria says while caressing his forehead. The infatuated couple cuddle in bed at first, and as their desire boils over once more, their two bodies fuse into one, and seemingly forever, they can't get enough of each other in their insatiable passionate crusade.

As Victoria sleeps, he kisses her on the forehead and contemplates her ethereal and placid beauty, and chuckles feeling wholesome. Right after, shortly before 6:00 a.m., he leaves the house.

Professor Cromwell-Smith rarely, if ever, jogs in the morning, but thanks to his newfound health, each passing day he feels stronger with plenty of energy to burn. Thus, today is an exception to his decades-old habit and routine of pedaling his old and rusty bike to the campus.

He has been running for more than an hour, through the hilly, tree-lined back campus roads. As he paces steadily mile after mile, the professor travels back in time visiting places of the heart that have been dormant for a long time – though never forgotten.

As the faculty buildings come into view, the longing hits him unexpectedly. Suddenly, even though Victoria is only a short distance away, he finds himself missing her. Shortly, he has to share with his class their courtship and life together. But, the long run and good sweat steadily calms him down. He is now ready, focused, and in the right frame of mind when he walks into class less than an hour later.

Royal Cambridge Scholastic Institute (2018)
(University's Auditorium)

"How's everyone today?" he asks aloud.

A pause follows, and then an unexpected collective response erupts.

"Insanely awesome!" the student body answers back in unison.

"Awesome!" he replies.

"Before we start, as this is a love story, please allow me to read you a fitting and profound overture to it," announces the professor as he starts to read in earnest.

"Of Fate and Fairy Tales"

Where does a fairy tale begin?

How does it start?

How is it created?

Where can we find one?

And once we do, how do we turn it on?

When is it that our life's pages,

shine and sparkle in all of their splendor,

and our hearts are suddenly filled

with magical dreams

and reciprocate love?

It is commonly said and acknowledged that fate is,

predictable, inexorable, ineludible,

inescapable, inevitable;

making us mere terrestrial beings

careening through the existential universe,

towards pre-planned destinations or outcomes.

Such a belief is not only false,

but it is crucially wrong

as it derails our spirits under the conviction

that our lives occur in some sort

of pre-ordained fashion.

But fate is just a banal excuse,

dressed under a fake historical costume

of legitimacy.

Its only purpose is to justify a non-deliberate life,

one that lacks meaning and purpose.

Fact is, we create our own fairy tales,

it is on us, no one else.

We can make a fairy tale out of anything,

anyone, or anywhere.

Life is a never-ending fairy tale if we make it such.

There is extraordinaire, magnificence, splendourness,

felicitousness and awesomeness,

around every corner, right in front of us,

as well as inside each one of us,

ready to be uncovered and released,

as long as we are able to see life and its people

with a touch of candor, ingenuity, and good faith.

And yet, there is nothing accidental or fortuitous about fairy

tales.

Many of us think that someday

we are going to run into

a fairy godmother, a wizard or an enchantress,

or even a prince on a white horse,

or a goddess of virtue, beauty, and strength,

that will sweep us off our feet.

What we have to realize though,

is that we are each one of those characters already,

as they all reside inside our own spirits.

So, how do we turn a fairy tale on?

First and foremost, with an unquenchable desire,

to live, love and dream.

Also,

by recognizing and appreciating

the inner beauty that resides in each human being,

no matter who they are.

And by understanding that,

no matter how dire they may be,

every circumstance, every moment,

every challenge, obstacle, or hardship,

no matter how unsavory they may seem;

every failure, defeat, or rejection,

no matter how deflating, they may appear;

they all have, not only existential value

but also enchantment,

for us to discover, enjoy, and experience.

Professor Cromwell-Smith finishes his overture in bliss, ready to take his class into a real fairytale. "As I said in our previous class, one of my mentors, back in Wales was an old lady antiquarian that I called Mrs. V. Spirited and cheerful, Victoria Sutton-Leigh was my biggest cheerleader and played a very important role in my life as I was growing up. When I wrote to her, breaking the news that I had fallen in love with Vicky, she wrote back asking what were the "little gestures" that had won me Victoria's heart? That is precisely where we will begin today - answering Mrs. V's questions, by returning to the place, in the sands of time, when Vicky and I fell in love.

"Today we are going to pick up the story at Mrs. V's antique bookstore, back in Wales, right after she receives my response to the request she made at the end of her last letter. It begins like this …"

Hay-On-Wye (1976)

(Mrs. V's Antique Book Store for the Young – Wales)

Mrs. V has been anxiously waiting for my response. The letter arrives on a fairly quiet Friday afternoon. The moment she sees the mailman arrive, she steps out and picks her correspondence up. Feeling all excited, she walks back to her shop in short steps. When Mrs. V recognizes my handwriting on one of the letters, a gigantic smile appears on her face, then in a hurry, she opens my missive and starts reading it, even before the startled mailman standing on the street has left her place.

Harvard (1976)

(Letter from Erasmus and Vicky to Mrs. V)

"Mrs. V you were right. I was so excited to tell you about winning her heart over that I skipped the whole story about how I did that. Please forgive me, but here it is, and this time I've left nothing out, not even Vicky, as both of us are narrating it to you," Erasmus writes to Mrs. V's delight, which is easily toppled by a big surprise as she realizes that the words that follow are from Vicky herself.

"Dear Mrs. V: Greetings from New England. I've heard so much about you. All of it wonderful. I want you to know, that I love Erasmus with all my heart. True love has indeed found us. I adore him. Mrs. V, you've done a marvelous job mentoring and shaping your endearing, precious boy. I sincerely hope to meet you in the future. Yours truly, Vicky - the enchantress that stole your beloved mentee's heart."

Mrs. V is deeply touched by Erasmus and Vicky's introductory words. She is also thrilled in anticipation to read the rest of the letter, but this does not prevent her from sticking to tradition — she walks over to her old Chesterfield where she spent countless hours reading to young Erasmus. Once comfy, she sets out to read in bliss. "Dearest Mrs. V, this is the story about how Vicky and I found the way to each other's heart. In the beginning, there are just little notes that I manage to drop here and there, always surprising her, while more often than not I am able to peek or glance at her reaction. However, it doesn't start out well as she reacts defensively, seemingly as if someone is trespassing on her private and hallow grounds. Yet, she never tears them up, which tells me that somehow her heart is listening. The second backlash comes in the form of utter rejection, as her reactions become cold and expressionless as if erecting a shield between her rational and emotional self. Little do I know that I am about to receive a huge existential lesson - that being defensive or aggressive in life is driven most of the time by fear and insecurity.

Note #1
(University Cafeteria)
"Your laughter makes me chuckle." Vicky turns her head and scouts the crowd without finding the culprit, then she folds the

handwritten note that was left on top of her diary. "This is not funny you guys, I'm nobody's clown," she complains to her classmates in the student-faculty cafeteria. Her statement is met with incredulous looks. Embarrassed, she stands up and leaves. Obfuscated, she does not pay attention to it at first, but curiosity still prevails before she tears up the intrusive and unwelcomed note. It begins with a glance, then her eyes become glued to the scribble written on the other side of the note:

"Life in Bliss"

"If you want to live life in bliss,

pay attention to the little details,

those that come straight from the heart,

those that are spontaneous gestures of love,

those that are just little things,

those that we offer and receive with absolute joy,

those that we never forget,

for the rest of our lives."

She carefully folds the note.

'It's a keeper,' she decides while shivering deep inside, as her dozing heart begins to wake up and there is nothing she can do about it.

Note #2
(University Library)

Vicky is laughing loud and nonstop. "He did it. He finally did it. Isn't that amazing? We should all be so proud of him," she proclaims to her classmates in the library. Everyone around her, high fives, embraces and celebrates the NFL drafting their college quarterback.

"Victoria, you should run for the student council as Miss Congeniality. It suits you better," a friend-rival classmate states. However, she is not paying attention as her eyes are intensely focused on the small yellow note.

"Your heart is noble and amazingly beautiful. Your spirit is fierce and loyal. Your soul is pure and innocent. You are an awesome woman."

"Who's the Romeo writing these notes? I don't find it funny at all!" she states to a non-responsive crowd while showing them the folded note, but still not sharing its contents.

A while later, sitting by herself, she can't wait to read the other side of the note. Part of her doesn't know what to think, but another part compels her to do so.

"Life is Not a Spectator's Sport"

Feeling good for long,

never happens to the bystander,

there is no success or achievement

as a spectator in life,

but only fun and intensity

which are only shallow and passing,

as the emptiness of a life without meaning,

will sink and settle,

when you are alone at night

with your own pillow.

Life to the contrary is a participant's sport,

a life where we are its main protagonists

and one where happiness

is not pursued but ensues,

as a result of our deliberate involvement

in a wholesome life experience."

'Who does he think he ...?' she mulls but stops midway through. 'He's right Victoria, whether you like it or not, he's right,' she reasons while the mystery about his identity, as well as her increasing heartbeat, continues to grow inside her at warp speed.

'His calligraphy is so beautiful,' she wonders while her eyes are glued to the magnificent artistry of the impeccably written note.

Note #3
(Ice Cream Parlor)

"How could anyone enjoy an ice cream so much? I love to feel the ecstasy in your face in the form of chocolate splashed all

over it. Happiness has a name and a face and it is you, Victoria."
She's alone when she discovers the note and chuckles at the
thought of her usual self, wearing ice cream plastered mouth to
cheeks. Then she joins her best friend, Gina, and as both are
about to leave the ice cream parlor, her heart jumps. She
recognizes him sitting in a booth by the corner, but he can't see
her as he is seated facing the street.

"Hi!" Victoria says, greeting him with a soft and yet warm
voice. Erasmus turns. She can sense his surprise, but as their
eyes lock, the pull hits them both in an instant. He remains
speechless and shell-shocked. She takes the lead.

"I meant to introduce myself days ago, but had not seen you
around for a while," she says trying to open up the conversation.
He tenses even more. She keeps on staring at him and then
blurts out, "I saw you looking at me that day from the stands,"
she says, referring to the first time he ever saw her marching as
a Harvard Band baton twirler during a football game opening
ceremony.

He starts to shiver inside when he hears it.

'So, it was mutual,' he realizes while remaining silent.

"My name is Victoria," she states flashing a happy face. He
hesitates once more as shyness completely seizes him, but to his
great relief somehow he manages to respond.

"I am Erasmus, nice to meet you," he blurts out with a sheepish
and nervous smile, but still remaining motionless as if nailed to

his seat. She stands right in front and stares at him, with big wide eyes that seem to be scrutinizing every inch and every gesture of the startled young man. Erasmus in turn looks at her with eyes filled with shyness and admiration. His stare is innocent and at the same time deep. Both remain motionless for what seems an eternity. The attraction is mutual, intense, and palpable, especially to their accidental witness, Gina, who is equally in awe and speechless. Unable to utter a single word, both youngsters have nevertheless connected to the deepest parts of each other's hearts. "See you around then," she says casually, turning around to leave in one continuous movement. In an instant, the two Harvard freshman girlfriends walk out to the street.

"A Brit? I love how proper English sounds coming from a man," Victoria wonders aloud while catching her breath.

"Victoria, who are you kidding? The accent? Who are you trying to fool? I've never seen you introduce yourself to anyone in here, quite the contrary, they chase you like flies," Gina states challenging her.

Again, Victoria is not paying any attention. She's going over each and every moment of the fortunate encounter. His gorgeous eyes, movie actor jaw, Hellenic nose, strong hands, masculine gestures, and deep voice. She's never felt this way before. 'He is gorgeous,' she mulls, trying to place who he reminds her of. Suddenly she freezes for a second as a chill seizes her. 'I got it, I got it, he is a younger version of Elizabeth Taylor's husband, the Brit she married twice – Richard Burton. Yes, that's him!' She rejoices in a whirlwind of emotions. Itching with curiosity Victoria peeks at the back of the note. She plans to read it later but can't resist and starts right away. The words immediately captivate her.

"Love's Rabbit Hole"

"How do you know when love
is knocking at your door?
You know it because when that someone unexpectedly erupts
into your life's journey,
it simply takes your breath away."

As the utter intensity of her feelings seizes her, Victoria's lower lip trembles at the realization. Her faint smile and incandescent eyes reflect a bit of fear with plenty of nascent love.

Note #4
(University Grounds After A Round of Frisbee)

As she is about to pick up her books from the park bench and head to class, Victoria sees the small note. "Wearing shoes of a different color makes you look vulnerable and absent-minded, something you are not, but it's overwhelmingly endearing as it candidly displays the child in you. I love it!" Tentatively she peeks down. Horror! How did it happen?

"Vic, I thought it was – you – making a fashion statement, girl you're losing it ... or perhaps it's a breeze coming all the way from across the Atlantic. Should we call it Brit love?" teases her best friend Gina.

"So you have nothing better to do than play cupid?" replies Victoria while she scans the grounds looking for him without any success.

"He's not here Vic. I already looked around. By the way, I don't think the Brit is writing the notes. I went back and I don't recall seeing him around when you got all the previous ones – except the other day at the ice cream parlor.

'It's true. Hopeless, wishful thinking of mine. My sleeping heart suddenly awakens into two totally different directions,' Victoria muses, yet to her great relief, she knows that the writing on the back of the latest note awaits her. Sure enough, as she reads it, Victoria is immediately thrown into places of the heart she doesn't ever want to leave.

"Love's Rabbit Hole" (cont.)

You know it, because,

when you can finally catch your breath,

all you inhale feels like at that moment,

there is absolutely nothing else

you would like to be doing,

nor is there anyone else in the world,

you would like to be with,

than your rabbit."

She chuckles while sighing.

'My rabbit?' she asks herself as she's more and more comfortable with the feeling. 'But I've got to find him first,' she reminds herself in a sudden reality check as she still doesn't have a clue who he is!

Note #5 and Gesture #1
(Student Dorms)

"Vic, you better come to the door," states Gina, as they are about to leave for class. On the floor at the doorstep of their dorm, there are three balloons and a narrow rectangular gift box. Taped to one of the balloon strings is a gigantic card with Victoria's name in big capital letters. Victoria hastily opens the card.

"So you never again confuse your shoes in the darkness as you leave early in the morning." She looks down and realizes that she is wearing one dark blue and one black loafer again. Horror! A burst of loud laughter can be heard as Gina realizes the mismatch as well.

"How could he have known?" asks a startled Vicky.

"Obviously, you've done it before or should I say often," states Gina mocking her.

Victoria opens the gift box and it contains a reading light.

47

"Who is this guy Gina? I've got to find out."

Wearing matching color shoes, she walks out of her dorm minutes later with a smile on her face. She loves the light and in fact has already used it. However, it's the back of the note that she craves the most. It doesn't take long for her to start reading it in earnest and sure enough, it does not disappoint.

Love's Rabbit Hole (cont.)

You know it,

when from the get-go,

you feel comfortable, confident

and light on your feet,

and life becomes a journey of two,

and soon after,

you become possessed

with this inexplicable certainty,

that you are safe, protected, and never alone."

'Who is he and why doesn't he show up?" she asks herself, as the need to know, burns throughout her entire being.

Note #6 and Gesture #2
(Student Dorms)

"Vic, the phantom of the camp strikes again," Gina announces in jest. Once more a surprise lies at their doorstep, this time in a cardboard takeaway tray. On it lie two coffees and a handful of fresh doughnuts. It's not only their favorite kind of breakfast but smells like heaven to the two freshmen. Again, the note does not disappoint.

"On Wednesdays, you are always running late because on Tuesdays you work until late at the homeless center. The next day you often miss breakfast."

"How does he know?" asks an incredulous Victoria.

"Because he cares, Vic."

This time an utterly joyous Victoria reads aloud the back of the note to Gina.

"Our Better Instincts of the Heart"

"In matters of love,

the brain and the heart are like oil and water,

they don't mix well together,

because the brain cannot

create, govern, control, or sustain love

and vice versa."

As they finish reading, both friends are left sitting together in their dorm room in silence while nodding their heads in full knowledge of what's exactly happening.

Victoria has finally fallen in love. The only problem though is that as of yet she still doesn't know who the guy is.

Note #7 and Gesture #3
(The Broken Baton)

On Friday, Erasmus travels overnight by train to New York City. He is at the store when it opens at 8:00 a.m. By 8:30 a.m. he is back at Penn Station and by early afternoon he is already in Boston.

In the meantime, Victoria has been extremely upset as her baton broke the previous day. Worst of all, when they finish rehearsing, Harvard's marching band leader apologizes and informs her that regrettably they would have to march without her that day. "Victoria, there is no point in you marching without your baton," he explains.

Dejected, she walks to her locker, quickly drops everything, turns around, and heads for the showers. Then, as she comes back wrapped in towels and feeling hopeless, something catches her attention. There's a package on top of her locker and her heart jumps as she recognizes the shape of the box. Involuntarily, while covering her face, she gasps. She reaches up and grabs the box – opening it with an exhilarating premonition. When the contents of the box are revealed, her heart stops and she cries softly, overcome by emotion. The card inside reads: "I tried to repair the broken one but I couldn't so I got you a new one. Victoria, our band is nothing without you." First, she picks up her broken baton from the box and while continuing to cry, she laughs at the mangled scotch tape holding it together. Then as she holds her brand new baton in absolute

50

awe and joy, she sees the back of the note and all her feelings bundle up inside, while she starts to read ...

"What is True Love?"

"True love is,

when your skin aches

without your other half's touch,

when nothing is warmer than being

in each other's arms,

True love is,

when your heart does not belong to you."

Right there and then all her instincts go array. She wants him. She needs him. She is taken and her heart is no longer hers. 'Let it be him please, let it be him,' she wishes with all her heart as she is torn between the Brit and the note writer but hopes that both are one and the same.

Note #8 and Gesture #4
(The Round Trip Trek)

Erasmus has been in the library for hours. Half the time tolling and the other half dreaming about seeing Victoria leading the marching band earlier that day with a huge smile and her brand new baton.

"Mr. Cromwell."

"Yes."

"Please follow me; we have an urgent long-distance call for you."

Erasmus snaps out of his daze and follows the middle age woman as she walks quickly ahead of him through the corridors of the ancient educational institution.

At the University's switchboard, he is directed to a telephone booth. "Lift the handset young man, your mother is on the line." He does as he is told in utter angst.

"Son, your father has had a heart attack and we're all at the hospital with him. I want you to know that he's getting the best possible care. He has asked about you on several occasions. Finally, about an hour ago, he pleaded with me to contact you and keep you informed. He loves you dearly son," states his mom with a broken voice.

"But how is he doing, mum? Will he be OK?"

"Son, he's very ill and may not make it. I will reach out to you again tomorrow morning with an update about his progress. Dear, if we could afford it, we would fly you home so that you could be with him at this moment, but you know that at present, we can't."

"I know mum, I know. Thank you for calling me. Don't spend any more money. I love you. I will be waiting for your call tomorrow and please tell him that I love him very, very much."

Erasmus hangs up and is in absolute turmoil. He decides to walk. Then, as the hours go by, he goes through a roller coaster of emotions and memories about his father. He gets lost in his own grief, and as he walks along the Charles River, he loses track of time and distance. By the time he comes back to his dorm, it's almost midnight. Somehow, he gets himself into bed and falls asleep. He dreams about his father throughout the night. At first, he only hears the persistent knock far away in the distance. Then, as he wakes up still half asleep, he remembers that his mother said she would call back. He heads to the door expecting to meet the same switchboard lady. As he checks the time, he sees that it's almost noon, but when he opens the door, there's no one outside. Did he just dream about it?

'I'll get ready quickly and head to the switchboard anyway,' he reasons in angst.

But as he starts to close the door, he sees it from the corner of his eye. There is an envelope on the floor and it contains a small note. Although still half asleep, he reads it expecting the worst. A state of ominous premonition and emotional exhaustion quickly creeps in and consumes him.

"Dear Erasmus, fly home and be with your father for as long as you need to." At first, he doesn't get it. Confusion is quickly followed by gratitude at the grand gesture until crude reality takes over... 'I wish I could but we can't afford it.' As he commiserates, he finally realizes the envelope's heaviness. He opens it. Then, as he reads it, his first reaction is one of total incredulity and shock.

"Oh my…" he blurts out.

The envelope contains a round trip airline ticket to London with a departure time in four hours. It also contains a train ticket to connect home upon arrival. Thirty minutes later, as he runs through the campus to his waiting cab, he almost crashes into a fellow student. When he recognizes that it's his best friend Matthew, he flashes a huge smile and bear hugs him.

"Thank you Matt, thank you," he yells but his friend is stiff as a board.

Matthew corrects him, "Erasmus, don't thank me, thank her. She turned this campus upside down to raise that money."

"What are you talking about? Who is she?" asks Erasmus, pleading with Matthew.

"Never mind, I can't tell you. Go home. Go see your dad," Matthew replies.

"But how did you guys find out?" asks a puzzled Erasmus.

"A faculty professor told us so that we could keep an eye on you. Man, just go, get going," Matthew answers while pushing him away.

Erasmus starts to run. He turns again asking his friend with body gestures.

"She's amazing, you're one lucky bastard, c'mon go, go home."

'Is it her? Who else could it be? Who else would care so much? It has to be her,' he tells himself with much hope.

Wales Regional Hospital, United Kingdom (1976)

"Mum!" Erasmus calls her as he walks into the hospital lobby. His mother turns around and sees him in the distance. Her tired and sleepless face lights up, followed by a big broad smile that seemingly erases her sad refrain. She quickly runs toward him overcome by emotion.

"My beautiful boy," she whispers while her effusive motherly embrace makes him feel safe and protected.

"How did you make it all the way here, son?" she asks with tears of joy running down her face.

"Someone who cares dearly, mum. It was a gesture that came out of a big, big heart."

"But who?"

"That, I still have to find out for sure when I get back."

They both tiptoe their way into his father's room.

"Father," he says softly while trying to wake him up.

An almost imperceptible squint follows and suddenly his father opens his eyes recognizing him at once. His eyes continue to widen and then remain fixated on Erasmus. A faint smile forms.

"Son."

Erasmus approaches the hospital bed and out of sheer impulse embraces his dad. He puts his arms around him and puts his head on his chest. They both cry a little and for a while, their intense bond of love is all they need from each other. "You don't know how much this means to me, son!"

Later that evening Erasmus learns how close his father came to passing away. But as the days go by, he improves faster than anyone ever expected. Soon, he's out of danger and hopefully on his way to a full recovery. Predictably, right away, his father starts urging him to go back to America. When Erasmus finally says goodbye to his parents, he realizes that it's the first time he has been on the streets and seen the light of day, since his arrival a week earlier. Then, while on the train back to London, he scolds himself for failing to contact his hometown antiquarian mentors as well.

Boston, MA (1976)
(Harvard University Dorms, Saturday 6 pm)

With his father on the mend, Erasmus arrives back in Boston a day before his 21st birthday – just in time, as a short getaway had been planned to celebrate his birthday. His plan is to take the train to the coast with a small group of friends; then the ferry for an overnight visit to Martha's Vineyard; then spend Sunday on bicycles wandering around the island's beaches. He has been obsessing about the identity of the woman that made it possible for him to visit his father. Who is she? He needs to know and has made plans to extract it from his friends over the weekend.

He hopes with all his heart for her to be the gorgeous baton twirler. Could she be the one?

'She hardly knows me. How could she care?' he tells himself trying to be realistic and rational. 'That's what you are - a perennial dreamer. But whoever she is, I've got to meet and thank her. Whoever she is, her heart is pure gold and has clearly won me over,' he quibbles. He stops dreaming for a second and reasons, 'perhaps she found out that it was me sending her the notes, poems, and baton!' He smiles in hope, but it doesn't last long as doubt quickly creeps back in.

'Be real Erasmus. Your infatuation is teetering on the edge of a delusional cliff.' He can't help it and is soon back to his obsession, 'how can you get anywhere with the beautiful baton twirler? You didn't even invite her over to celebrate your birthday.' He knows it's only a lame excuse, but he tries to convince himself that she wouldn't have been able to come anyhow, as Harvard's football team had a game on the road earlier in the day four hundred miles away.

Harvard Marching Band Bus
8 p.m. Saturday (100 miles away from Boston)

Vicky, you don't know what you're doing anymore," states Gina referring to the air ticket grand gesture that Victoria put together.

"I know I'm acting on impulse Gina, but I feel happy. I'm just following my heart."

"And you have. Getting him that ticket was awesome, but what's he done for you?"

"I don't know and I don't care. I just have this uncontrollable desire to protect him."

"You're still fixated that he's the Brit phantom of the dorms! I told you that he can't – he couldn't be."

"Then who is he?"

"Let him surface girl, let him show himself and then you'll know if he's your prince charming."

"Do you know what coach told me? He said that whoever got me the baton had to go all the way to New York City overnight to get it," states Victoria.

"Yeah, that was an amazing gesture, and I would be head over heels as well for the guy, as you are," Gina finally admits, but her sharp tongue still has more to say. "The problem Victoria is that you're trying to fit a Brit square peg into a magnificent round hole. They don't fit."

Victoria starts to tear up and Gina backs off, trying to support her best friend. "About your latest crazy idea, I'm going to go on your weekend trip, if only to protect you from yourself," states a supportive Gina.

Martha's Vineyard
Sunday Morning (1976)

It is 7:00 a.m. and the small group of Harvard students is out of their cozy Bed and Breakfast and on bikes heading toward the picturesque city center. It's only a short visit as almost everything is closed at such an early hour - all they want is sand and water! They zigzag through different beaches where they splash, run, sunbathe, and race against each other on their bikes. By noon they are crusty from the sand, saltwater, island winds, and a hefty dose of the spring sun. They have a reservation for lunch at 12:15 p.m. at a small seafood restaurant back at city center. That's where they plan to cut the cake for the birthday boy. The restaurant turns out to be a family place packed with customers. The group gets seated and starts laughing at the stunt that two of them, Matthew and Greg, pulled at a deserted beach on the southwest side of the island. Both of them got totally naked and ran from the sand dunes to the water.

"The two of you look awful naked. Your pale, milky almost translucent skin, after just a bit of sun seems more like a lobster tail," states Erasmus as all laugh in unison.

Gesture #5
(The Martha's Vineyard Magic Moment)

Suddenly, two hands cover his eyes from behind. The movement is slow and deliberate, caressing and tender.

"Hi," she whispers in his ear sending a chill up and down his spine. He gets an instantaneous knot in his throat. Soon he's trembling all over. Then, the unexpected happens, he turns and holds her face with both hands and for a brief moment, that seems like an eternity, they hold each other's faces with the palms of their hands, staring at one another with such intensity that the world around them seems to disappear. Erasmus then gently draws her face closer and kisses her with passion. She responds and soon they get lost in each other.

"Hey, can you guys interrupt your wonderful love dream, or should I say open-ended kiss, so we can cut the cake and get the hell out of here?" states Gina in typical fashion.

After the brief ceremony, Gina, who accompanied Victoria on the trip, takes Erasmus' friends back to Boston and the young couple stays over in Martha's Vineyard. They stroll around the island, chat and laugh, share smiles and dump their entire lives on each other, and yes, they continue to kiss and embrace as if there is no tomorrow. Then, on an empty beach, they make love for the very first time, lost in their own world filled with passion and desire. It is clumsy and inexperienced lovemaking, but it is beautiful and delicate, uninhibited, and amazingly harmonic as if they had been together for years.

But there is yet more to come, as the night is about to grant them one more magical moment. It starts as a whisper, and at first, she can't figure it out. He looks at her with dreamy eyes as his voice starts to make sense while repeating the same phrase over and over again.

'Is he improvising, perhaps looking for a rhyme?' she wonders in awe ... then it happens as his voice starts to make sense, it begins through a cascade of words of art and inspiration.

"My Radiant Goddess of the Night"

Here we are

under a star-studded sky,

in the silence of the night,

over the moist

but still warm sands

of an empty beach.

Here we are on this magic island,

where our story,

the one that is only about the two of us,

has begun.

My Wicked Lady of the Night,

where are you taking me?

Where are you taking us

with this nascent love?

When I see you,

I sigh in joy,

just with your presence.

When you look at me

my infatuated heart,

makes me tremble.

Just one touch or a slight brush

from that warm silky skin of yours

makes me moan all over

in ecstasy-filled desire.

And when you embrace me

I feel this inexplicable plenitude,

a blissful certitude,

that I am at a safe harbor,

protected and no longer alone.

My radiant Goddess of the Night,

where are you taking us?

Where are you taking me

with this nascent love of mine?

Victoria shivers with intense joy before drowning in an endless kiss of gratitude for her other half.

Late at night, they doze off leaning on each other while on the train back to Boston; the young couple exudes plenitude as an aura of utter happiness hovers over them. Their enamored faces glitter with nascent love. They look completely at ease and totally comfortable with one another.

Her sudden rhetorical question teases him off his delightful dream.

"Tell me it is you. It's got to be you. Tell me, tell me please!" Her plea derives straight out of her infatuated heart.

Erasmus knows perfectly well that she knows the answer. Yet he succumbs to her improvised charade filled of sweet enthusiasm.

He smiles while ever so slightly nodding. Impetuously, she jumps all over him.

"I knew it! I knew it! Her words erupt between kisses in a state of exuberant euphoria.

"And, shall I presume that you were the guardian angel that made it possible? Enabling me to make it all the way to Wales?" he teases in return.

"And brought you back as well; don't you forget that," she replies in jest although with a possessive-celebratory tone. The two of them stare at each other in joyful complicity. The last sound that can be heard before their arrival is both of them cracking the loudest of laughter; its echoes spreading like a wildfire racing out of two incandescent hearts.

Boston Main Train Station (1976)

Their train's arrival in Boston causes a slight intermission to their never-ending kiss. They walk away from the train station holding hands, which from then on is their custom when walking together.

They become hopelessly inseparable and in a few weeks, they move in together. A poetic overture soon follows as Erasmus creates for his love a verse she later calls, "Irresistible." He delivers it by reading it as they step into their newly rented studio for the very first time.

"There is Something About You"

Ever since that day we met,
there is something about you,

63

that makes life magical.

Don't ask me how,

but it is this irresistible

and wickedly beautiful spell you cast,

that simply makes us happy, whole, and safe.

There is something about you,

that colors everything

and makes every sunrise,

a wonderful beginning,

and every sunset,

not only a glorious end but also,

a continuous spin with a new beginning.

There is something about you,

that always feels anew.

There is something very special about you,

that makes love come alive,

and one twinkles, shivers, and breathes deep

with a smile.

There is something about you,

that enraptures my heart,

and makes it forever yours.

"Welcome to the journey," Erasmus is barely able to say as his impetuous baton twirler drowns him in hugs and kisses as they hurriedly walk back to their new bedroom where a world of non-stop love and passion awaits them.

"Hay-On-Wye (1976)"
(Mrs. V's Antique Book Store for the Young – Wales)

Mrs. V sits on her Chesterfield while gently rocking in a state of profound joy and pride for her beloved mentee. Erasmus and Vicky's letter sits on her lap and the tips of her tiny fingers keep on caressing it as if she was holding a treasure, while almost imperceptibly tapping it as if she was typing and sending a message to them to help preserve and protect their true love forever.

"Royal Cambridge Scholastic Institute" (2018)
(University's Auditorium)

The professor stares at his class for what seems like an eternity, his eyes far away in the past. Slowly, he comes back with a deeply melancholic smile. He then scans the room and sees more than a few teary faces, but recognizes that like his, they are all tears of happiness.

"There are instances in life where we are blessed with immense and wholesome joy; most of them are unexpected bends in the road. But, when they do occur, be ready to seize the moment and ensure that you do not let it slip, or miss a single beat, as these are not only rare opportunities that come far and few in between in life, but neither do we know how long they will last or if they will ever show up again."

"Class, I will see you next week and I will take you back to a memorable day when Vicky and I met a very special lady that would become a very important part of our lives – class dismissed."

"I want to fall in love like that," states a dreamy-eyed energetic young brunette that never liked poetry before joining his class.

"Who wouldn't want to have someone that steals your heart away, and takes you into the land of the happy hearts? Who wouldn't want that?" breathes out a tall red-haired girl, captain of the volleyball team, while wishing life to present her with her own true love fairytale.

CHAPTER 3

"LIFE, CHARACTER AND VIRTUE"

Royal Cambridge Scholastic Institute (2018)
(Erasmus and Victoria's Campus Home)

"Come here my irresistible Brit." While staring intensely at him, Victoria slowly lifts the corner of the warm and cozy bed comforter, enticing him to squeeze in. As if hypnotized, Erasmus dutifully complies, wearing an expression of joyful obedience and plentitude at being commandeered.

"What am I going to do with you?" she asks with a tease mixed with a playful false pretense.

"Anything you may desire, my lady," he obliges already burning with desire. Later on, as Vicky opens her eyes, the first things that come into view are his smile and her favorite treat, freshly squeezed orange juice.

"You always manage to get me out of my innate morning grumpiness," she complains while feeling happily spoiled.

"Erasmus, where are you taking your students today?" she asks, as they sit down for breakfast.

"Back to the day you and I met Mrs. Peabody." With a dreamy look, Victoria seems to drift away into the distance, and then absentmindedly blurts out, "quite a day dear, quite a day. To me, she will always be Mrs. P."

"Good old Mrs. P indeed," he replies.

"Royal Cambridge Scholastic Institute" (2018)
(University's Auditorium)

Professor Cromwell-Smith is totally lost in memories of the past as well when not long after, he walks into a packed auditorium. He doesn't quite know how he made it into the classroom. 'Surely my adaptive subconscious navigated me here,' he mumbles to himself unconvincingly trying to justify his acute absentmindedness.

"How's everyone today?" asks an enthusiastic professor.

"Insanely awesome!" replies a spirited student body.

With a slight nod of gratitude and respect, the pedagogue is eager to start.

"From a very early age, I gravitated towards the world of books. Accordingly, my first true friends and mentors were three antiquarians from my hometown in Wales. Well, serendipity struck. While living with my newfound love, Vicky, in Boston, the same thing happened, but this time with New England antiquarians. The first antiquarian was an unforgettable and sweet lady we met by accident, literally stumbling into her shop, while on a long bike ride, wandering around the Northern shore of Massachusetts."

"Today, we will revisit that memorable day by going back in time. It starts like this."

Harvard (1976)

Having fallen madly in love, Vicky and Erasmus have been living together for a couple months. Quite comfortable with each other from the beginning, they have already settled into a series of routines that fit both their inclinations and preferences. During the week, besides their academic duties, they both work as tutors. So, when the weekend comes they take full advantage of their free time. One of their favorite pastimes is to be on their bikes for hours. On weekends they take them along as they get on a train going anywhere within the state. They get off at random places, sometimes along the coastline. Other times, they get off deep within the Massachusetts countryside. Once they get on their bikes, they usually ride 40 to 50 miles through some of the cutest little towns and small villages to be found in America. At day's end, exhausted, they crash at any of the countless Bed and Breakfasts across the state.

This particular weekend starts like most of the others with an early train ride on Saturday morning, along with their picnic basket and bikes, to Manchester by the Sea. Their plan is to ride alongside the coastline through Gloucester, Rockport, Newbury and end up at Sand Point on Plum Island. Then, they will find a place to spend the night and take an early train back to Boston on Sunday morning. Their idyllic escapade starts as they hop on their bikes. Soon they are engulfed by the sounds of the birds, the ocean, the pastel colors sprinkled along the New

England countryside, and the aroma of the sea. It's so idyllic and halcyon. After wonderful sightseeing at Halibut Point and Cape Ann, they jaunt into the tiny enclave of Lanesville.

Lanesville, Massachusetts (1976)

As soon as they peddle into the picturesque village, their eyes are drawn to a postcard-perfect storefront that advertises itself as: "Peabody & Co., Antique Books" (est. 1890). Erasmus is immediately transfixed. Victoria would later describe his reaction as if the world had suddenly disappeared, including her, and nothing else mattered.

When entering Peabody & Co., the first thing that any visitor will run into is the biggest, broadest smile and most spontaneous, thunderous laughter one could ever witness – that of one Eleanor Peabody-Smith. Even though there are no straight angles to be found, as every bit of her is round in nature, Mrs. P still moves her portentous frame with ease. She's from a distinguished New England family and her family roots date all the way back to the eighteenth century. She was very young when she married her first love and enjoyed an idyllic life until ten years into her childless marriage she lost her husband tragically at sea in a heavy storm. Since then, and after a brief but unfulfilling experience within the law profession, her love in life became her antique bookstore.

Young Erasmus is in a trance as he scopes the stacks upon stacks of books lying all around. His mouth is ajar and his eyes denote awe and wonder. Then, as Mrs. Peabody approaches, she states, "Who do I have the pleasure of welcoming on this beautiful morning at my humble place of enlightenment?"

Vicky seems startled and can't control her enthusiasm as she absorbs the magnitude of the number and shape of the old books around her. Also, the smell hits her right away. 'What is it? Old leather or paper? Or perhaps a bit of both?' Vicky reflects.

'The smell of erudition and knowledge?' Vicky muses. The store is a mess and yet Vicky senses order in chaos. 'This store is an exact reflection of its owner. Everything is in plain sight on both counts, the antiquarian and her books. I'll bet she can find anything in here in a split second,' Vicky concludes.

'A young beautiful couple interested in my antique books, what am I missing?' Mrs. P mulls over. An unrhetorical question, you silly.'

All three are all lost in their thoughts when Mrs. Peabody brings them all back to reality.

"Make yourselves comfortable. May I offer you something to drink – perhaps a freshly brewed iced tea?" she offers.

Erasmus declines. Iced drinks, much less tea of all things, are something he has not yet become accustomed to.

'What is it? With all of this ice consumed by Americans, you would think they would freeze their throats," Erasmus mulls in typical European fashion.

"Howdy, I am Erasmus."

"I am Victoria."

"Well, well, I am Eleanor, Eleanor Peabody-Smith."

"Brit?" Mrs. P asks.

"Wales."

"Where in Wales?"

"Hay-on-Wye."

"It figures," she says flashing her huge smile again.

"Also known as "Book Town," the mecca of antique bookstores. That explains it all," Mrs. Peabody reasons voicing her thoughts.

Erasmus smiles sheepishly acknowledging her compliment.

"What about you Victoria, Midwest?"

"Yep, Waterloo, Southwestern Illinois."

"I see, a twosome made out of the new and the old world," states the bubbly antiquarian.

"Mrs. Peabody, he doesn't drink anything with ice," Victoria clarifies.

"How silly of me, I'll spare the ice then, but only for him right?" she says winking at Vicky.

"Young man, what on earth could my modest book piles have for a resident of the antiquarians' citadel in Wales?" she asks as she fixes the drinks.

The self-absorbed Erasmus does not react. He's in a trance.

'He's in his element. This is his passion,' Vicky reflects.

In the meantime, Erasmus contemplates Mrs. Peabody's high-wired body language with total delight.

"You remind me of Mrs. V back home." His remark is intimate and warm, spoken with the easiness and comfort of someone with his defenses completely down.

"Is that so, tell me about her then," Mrs. P replies reacting emphatically as she clicks and connects with Erasmus' candid gesture of affection.

Erasmus still does not answer as he continues to stare at Mrs. P while visualizing his stalwart steward, Mrs. V, back at home. Realizing he's in one of his absent-minded spells, Vicky steps in to fill the void once more.

"He literally grew up, inside his hometown's antique bookstores and some of the owners became his life-long mentors. It all started way back when he was just eight years old. Mrs. V is one of them. Her name is Victoria Sutton-Raleigh.

"Mrs. V is …" the grand and overly effusive lady interrupts with a smile of realization. "Sutton-Raleigh antique books for the children. The best of its kind. She's a war widow from a wealthy Wales family, isn't she?" asks an emotional Mrs. P while mumbling non-stop.

Vicky turns to Erasmus looking for an answer.

"Yes, she is," he blurts out.

"Well, I've dealt with her over the years. She is prompt, diligent, and dependable. You see, periodically I receive orders for antique children's books and I get them all by mail from her."

Erasmus' excitement grows as he listens. He comes back to earth. He's suddenly ready to re-engage, although in a totally unrelated topic.

"Mrs. Peabody, I recently finished reading Benjamin Franklin's autobiography and fell in love with his dissertations about character and virtue. I am wondering if you have anything about that subject?"

"As a matter of fact I do, my son."

Mrs. P's agility around the book "pile-on" is a spectacle more worthy of admiration than emulation. One second she is atop a feeble ladder moving books and searching and soon after she is kneeling down looking further, then apparently remembering. Next, she is walking resolutely down the aisle straight to one spot where she lifts with ease an enormous book that she hand-carries with both arms as if cradling it. She then places it, on what used to be a large dining table, now packed with ancient books that she briskly pushes around to give herself more room to open the enormous book.

Mrs. Peabody opens the book right in the middle and Vicky is quickly initiated into the world of antique books. She can now see firsthand the cloud of dust and the smell of old paper and leather in the air.

"I've got something here that although seems and feels old, it was only recently written, but it is quite worthy of Mr. Franklin's words on character and virtue. Let me read it to both of you," states Mrs. P while clearing her throat.

"Life, Character and Virtue"

One's character is <u>our calling card</u> to life,

as well as,

the legacy our wake leaves behind.

Our character <u>defines</u>

not who we think we are,

much less what we pretend to be,

but who we really are deep, deep inside.

Our character is <u>respected</u> when,

we show immutable honesty and steadfast frankness.

Our character is <u>emulated</u> when,

we are uncompromisingly ethical,

approach everything with unquestionable rectitude,

indomitable integrity

and behold a spirit with purpose

and a soul with meaning.

Our character is <u>revered</u> when in possession of,

limitless compassion, unmaterialistic generosity

and the humblest of all wisdom.

Our character becomes <u>reliable</u> through,

dependable and immanent self-discipline.

Our character grows through,

unyielding perseverance, unrelenting grit,

unflinching resilience

and the insatiable pursuit of insight, knowledge,

and spirituality.

Our character is genuine only when,

we perennially put into practice,

inescapable forgiveness of one's self and others,

coupled with a readiness to rectify

and learn from our mistakes.

Our character is revealed as to what

we are really made of

when demanded and required by life

and its circumstances

which may involve abnegation, sacrifice,

and even relinquishment,

as the ultimate test about the fiber and nature,

our hearts are made of.

Our character perennially renews itself,

and remains crystalline through,

unstained innocence, unpremeditated candor,

joyful spontaneity and boundless ingenuity.

Our character builds a legacy with,

Never-ending and bountiful deeds, empathetic

and mindful judgment,

unbreakable courage, unwavering effort,

undeterred resoluteness,

relentless pace, obsessive zeal, unwandering firmness,

unleashed talent, incomparable and unmatched ability,

opportune impulsiveness

and unfettered ingeniousness.

Our character <u>transcends</u> when,

we are "ready to be" or "forever are" in love

with life, everyone

and our true love with sustained passion.

Being alive presents us with countless paths that,

in <u>the pursuit of moral excellence,</u>

<u>elevate our character</u> to its pinnacle,

and produce a state of unrepentant virtuosity.

When Mrs. Peabody finishes, Erasmus and Vicky are holding their hands tightly, as if they're sharing energy absorbed from the force and strength of the words they've just heard. They're both visibly shaken by the power of the old scribble. Soon, questions start to form, but their parallel thoughts are interrupted by their mind reader host.

"Character and virtue are not God-given gifts that you are born with. To the contrary, they require hard and persistent work in order to build, grow, acquire and preserve them," states Mrs. P finally showing her scholarly persona.

"Always remember this, your virtues define your character, and your character defines your legacy," Mrs. Peabody concludes.

"Thank you Mrs. … can we call you Mrs. P?" Victoria asks.

Eleanor Theresa Peabody-Smith flashes her signature smile once more.

"Of course you may, dear."

"Then again, thank you, Mrs. P," the young and grateful couple state in unison before resuming their cycling trek along the New England coastline.

Royal Cambridge Scholastic Institute (2018)
(University's Auditorium)

Professor Cromwell-Smith brings his class back to the present with a broad smile as if imitating Mrs. P.

"Class, Mrs. Peabody called upon us to realize the crucial importance of character and virtue. Over time, the memorable sessions with her grew in importance in both our lives and helped us build character and strength," states the professor.

"Always remember this, character sits at the confluence between what others think and what we really think, deep down inside, about ourselves. Virtues, on the other hand, besides being an essential component of a wholesome character, not only need to be acquired and developed but are at the same time, the essential life tools we depend on, in order to overcome, sustain, outlast and endure our existence," adds Cromwell-Smith bringing the class to a close.

"He is definitely a new man," comments a regular in his classes. "Absolutely! His enthusiasm and passion are through the roof," adds a tall brunette student.

"He's also giving us more of himself. His current classes are almost twice the length of his earlier sessions," states one of his most ardent followers as they all contemplate the lanky figure as he pedals away on his old rusty bike.

"It's all a matter of love. It's that simple. He's truly happy for the first time in many years," reflects the leader of the web-based forum about Cromwell-Smith's classes.

CHAPTER 4

SNAP OUT OF IT

Royal Cambridge Scholastic Institute (2018)
(Erasmus and Victoria's Campus Home)

"Time to wake up," he whispers. His voice is tender and filled with love. Victoria feels the warm air of his breath. She smiles with her eyes closed and in one single move, she wraps her arms around him.

"Got you my prince valiant," she blurts in desire. She pulls him closer until their skin is tightly compressed to one another. He is so warm that it makes her tremble. Her legs and arms curl around him and she squeezes until their bodies seem to fuse into one. Victoria radiates immense happiness, while Erasmus exudes a never-ending satiated smile.

(Campus Backroads)

Some days they bike, others like today, they walk. Victoria's arm is wrapped around Erasmus as she leans on him, with her head resting on his shoulder. Today, they have been strolling in slow motion for over an hour along the campus's tree-lined streets. Already, the beginning of the fall shows itself with a slightly chilly breeze. The temperatures are in the low 50's and the magnificent New England fall colors show themselves as leaves have been dropping all over the place.

As they huddle against the wind, their destination comes into view. That's when Erasmus finally makes a decision about his subject matter for the day's class.

"Vicky, do you remember the time when I was constantly obsessing about everything?" Erasmus asks as they are about to arrive at his classroom building.

"How couldn't I? Sometimes you were driving both of us crazy."

"Do you remember what we did to remedy that?"

For a moment Vicky pauses and hesitates but soon after, smiles.

"That was a fortunate set of circumstances," she replies with fond memories.

"Indeed they were Vic. Indeed they were," he says in affirmation.

"Mr. L?" she blurts out.

"That's right Vic, Mr. L" he exclaims all excited.

They have now arrived and Erasmus kisses Vicky good-bye. She gives him a tiny, little push that sends him into poetic overdrive.

"My love, that memorable encounter turned out to be the perfect prescription for your occasional obsessive fits. What a wonderful gift you have for your class today. Be the best you can be, my inspired poet."

Today, Professor Cromwell-Smith has an extra spring in his step. After all, the true love of his life has just sent him into class, in a noble state of mind and spirit.

Royal Cambridge Scholastic Institute (2018)
(University's Auditorium)

The auditorium is all waiting when the professor steps in whistling. For a brief moment, he contemplates his class with intensely pensive eyes.

"How's everyone this morning?"

"Ready professor," states a bunch of the students.

"Awesome," voices another group as he is ready to start.

"More often than not, we are our own worst enemies. Somehow, somewhere, we manage to get in our own way – sabotaging our existential roads and paths. Today I'll take you to a time where an eccentric antiquarian taught us a great lesson about how to avoid self-defeating behaviors."

"There was a time back at my Harvard days when I was driving everyone crazy. I would get fixated on something that caught my attention and soon after I would be so immersed in it that the world and its people, including Vicky, became secondary, even unimportant. Day after day I found myself, constantly and increasingly, testing everyone's patience, limits and boundaries that is, until an unforgettable day, changed everything."

"It started like this …"

Harvard (1976)

Harvard and Yale's rivalry is classic and never-ending because it refuels itself every year when the two institutions compete at every level. As results alternate over time, there is never a clear winner between the two. Of the fierce rivalries, that pit one against the other, the fiercest is football.

New Haven, Connecticut (1976)

On this weekend, Erasmus and Vicky, travel to Yale University, New Haven, Connecticut, as Harvard is playing on Yale's turf. Erasmus sits in the stands while Harvard's baton twirler, Victoria, leads the band with her usual high energy and joy. As Erasmus sees her from afar, he becomes notoriously smitten by the sweet elixir of true love. No matter how pretty, how much energy, charisma, and joy she normally exudes, today she excels even more, looking prettier and exhibiting an exuberant and sparkling enthusiasm. But, above all else, she looks extremely happy.

The two love birds are on a two-day trip. As soon as her duties are over, Victoria and Erasmus head into town. A French movie playing at the Shubert Theatre on College Street catches their eye. It is called "Les Unes et Les Autres" (the ones and the others) directed by Claude Lelouch with music by Michelle Legrand. It is a "Tour De Force" filled with ballet, classic music, and jazz, and an allegory to the lives of Rudolf Nureyev, Glenn Miller, and Wernher Von Karajan. Vicky and Erasmus huddle together as they enjoy the movie and it becomes one of their all-time favorites. It has such an impact that the two start to fall under the spell of the magnificent French culture. But, a couple in love can often miss the writing on the wall.

Fortunately, even fatefully, right away another clue surfaces just across the street. "Erasmus look, a Boulangerie & Bistro. Why don't we get a bite?" As they sit in the tiny eatery on small and cozy chairs with an even smaller table, Vicky opens up.

"In my hometown, we have a Boulangerie like this one, so I grew up with freshly baked real French bread and pastries," she says thrilled and orders right away.

"We want a couple of warm croissants, crispy on the outside and flaky inside, strawberry or orange marmalade, French butter on the side, and two cafe-au-lait, please. Ah, before I forget, please bring us a -pain au chocolat- for us to share. Thank you."

Right in front of a startled Erasmus, Vicky has just spit-fired the food order, giving no room for anything else to be considered – not even the natural sequence of the meal dishes, as they end up having dessert first.

"This is like a ritual to you Vic?" states an amused Erasmus. She just chuckles, but that's her and he loves it, as well as the croissants, especially when they are like heaven in his mouth. He counts twenty-plus different kinds of freshly baked bread in the display case. Then she orders their main course which consists only of a soup, a -bouillabaisse- and even though it sounds meager, this is the mother of all pottages. It's delicious, filling, and slow to process which is fine as in between, they chat and laugh and are inside their own little world. Then it happens, through the window, Erasmus sees a series of belt-driven ascending trays, about a foot apart. But what catches his attention are the books lying on each one of the trays. When Vicky sees the obsessive expression on his face, alarm bells go off.

'Oh boy, what is it this time?' she thinks.

She then turns towards the window and it registers.

"Dear, those are …?"

"Antique books, Victoria," replies Erasmus while waiving toward the waitress.

` "We need to find out why such valuable books are being carried up in this peculiar fashion," he wonders aloud.

"Excuse me, those books are being lifted where?" an exultant Erasmus asks the waitress. She smiles as if the question had been asked of her thousands of times before.

"That's Mr. Lafayette's store cargo elevator. A clever way to catch the attention of visitors like you, hoping some will become actual clients," the waitress explains.

"He sells antique books?" asks the startled and incredulous Vicky.

"Lafayette Antique Books has been around for one-hundred-fifty years. It was founded by his great grandfather in New York

City. Mr. Lafayette moved here a few years ago after selling the original store, as rental property in New York City became too costly. So, when he came into town, he bought this building. But just before setting the store up top, he decided to rent the ground floor to us to bring traffic into the building. Many people have tried to buy this property, but he won't sell."

The soup is half-finished when Erasmus quickly drops a ten-dollar bill, takes Vicky's hand, and marches her out of the eatery. He walks hastily around the building until he finds the stairs and starts to climb in hurried steps, literally dragging her along. Then as they reach the top, he sees the store sign: "Lafayette Antiquarians. The finest antique books in town (Est. 1867)."

"Vic, we would've never known of this place if not for your desire for crispy and flaky croissants with real French marmalade and butter," he blurts out as they enter the store.

"Vic, this is not a coincidence. Everything is Gallic today!"

The store is stunning and classic. It's also enormous in size and height. From floor to ceiling, the rooms are impeccably framed in mahogany and oak. Every book on every shelf is perfectly lined and stacked. Even the scent of the place is distinctively different. The air does not feel dusty and heavy but purified with the smell of gardenias and roses. "It feels like a private library in an English manor," states Erasmus in awe of his surroundings.

"I've never seen anything like this in my life. To me, this place is like a book museum," replies the inexperienced and candid Vicky, who is a bit lost with the overwhelming display of ancient scribbles. They first see him sitting by the window on a sofa, next to a brass floor lamp that projects a unique halo of intense and bright light on him. He's smoking in small puffs out of a curled classic pipe. He's totally absorbed in the book in front of him. As they approach, they can faintly hear music playing. The music is a classic French song from a powerful female voice, singing from the top of her lungs, with a strong emphasis on the "sliding Rs", something common in French songs from that era.

"That's Edith Piaf," says Erasmus without thinking and simply reacting to his childhood memory banks of countless hours around his Francophile diminutive mentor from Wales, dear old Mrs. V. "One of the great, perhaps the best, French female singers of all time," he adds.

When the store master finally notices the young couple, as if embarrassed by being caught off guard, he stands up abruptly. Then, after the first glance at his potential clients, he stiffens even more as if his expectations have been suddenly deflated. Now fully erect, his height comes into evidence.

'He must be 6'5" to 6'6" tall,' thinks Erasmus.

He has Mediterranean looks with slightly tanned skin, jet black hair, and deep green eyes. Piedmont Lafayette, a Columbia graduate in arts and literature, with two grown-up children, has been married for thirty years to a French ballet dancer. A natural athlete in his youth, excelling at soccer and basketball, he was on his way to the NBA when a knee injury derailed his career. But he didn't remain idle for long. He soon fell in love with the world of antique books, thus, continuing a family tradition.

"Welcome, may I be of any help?" he states cautiously with a baritone voice.

"We're in town for the football game," Erasmus replies in a trance.

"Harvard?" he asks confirming his first impression that the youngsters aren't clients but just visitors that are going to waste his time.

'These two have no clue about the value of books, especially those as old as the ones I have here,' he thinks in exasperation already trying to figure out how to get rid of them.

Vicky senses the undertones building inside the giant antiquarian and judges him better than he's judging himself.

'Bad luck! We couldn't have come at a worse moment. I'll bet he hasn't had a client in hours. So, we're going to be the sole recipients of his frustration as he has already realized that we won't be buying anything,' Vicky reflects with absolute accuracy.

But Erasmus is in another world, completely oblivious to the mundane nuances of body language and the oversized mercantile ego of their host. So, as usual, he marches forward before Vicky is able to warn him.

"Perhaps you have something about freeing one's spirit of its filters and roadblocks?" asks Erasmus staring intensely at Victoria, as if he is putting out an unsolicited opinion of himself. The tall man's rictus now turns into disbelief and surprise.

"Excuse me!" interrupts Vicky, impulsively caught up in the moment. Both men turn their attention to her and the tone of her voice. "What about something to get you out of situations that may obsess and obfuscate you. Something about how to stop such behavior," she blurts out, nailing what Erasmus wants to say, though with a slightly accusatory tone.

Now Vicky and Mr. Lafayette both stare at Erasmus, but he still doesn't get it, not even one bit, as he continues to look straight forward, his eyes fixated and totally focused on his request.

In the meantime, the eccentric antiquarian's persona has now changed to curiosity and interest.

"Kids, I am not a counselor. I sell precious and ancient books." He immediately sees the dejected expressions on both their faces and this gets to him.

"All right, why don't we start from the beginning. Why would you expect an antique bookstore to be a place for counseling?"

he asks with a newfound warm tone of affection that serves as an icebreaker, at least for a brief moment.

"We're not seeking counseling per se. We just want to look at and maybe read a few of your manuscripts," states a still determined Erasmus trying to be assertive.

"Then why didn't you just ask?" he says brusquely. His grumpiness has virtually vanished as he reverses course for good.

"Is this something you habitually do, I mean, going to antique bookstores to read?" asks a now willing and amused, but a bit uncertain antiquarian.

A pause follows. Once more Vicky jumps to the rescue of her absent-minded, taciturn boyfriend.

"He's done precisely that all of his life," Vicky intercedes once again.

"Is that so?" is Lafayette's remark of acknowledgment and respect to a fellow member of the exclusive club of readers of antique books. "Why not say so at first?" Lafayette declares.

'Perhaps he is a gifted youngster,' the antiquarian reasons trying to reset his thinking.

"Mr. Lafayette, I gather?" asks Vicky, taking the initiative away from the tall antiquarian and starting from the beginning.

"That's right, who do I have the pleasure?" he asks, easing up even more, now with the tone of a man with a mission.

"Victoria and Erasmus, sir," she states quickly, eager to make her next point.

The big man nods his head in deference with an expression of continuous curiosity on his face.

"Erasmus comes from Hay-on-Wye," she suddenly and instinctively blurts out.

Mr. Lafayette is surprised, already in a trance.

'There you have it, satisfied now?' he mulls over, scolding himself.

"And he has grown up inside these type of places, of course he has," Mr. Lafayette states completing the sentence with heartfelt pleasure and a big smile on his face.

"And the store owners have been his lifetime mentors," Vicky adds promptly.

"All right then, young Victoria and Erasmus, what were you both inquiring about earlier?" He asks as he takes big strides away from them.

'He knows exactly what to look for, he is a very attentive listener even if he seems not to be,' Vicky reflects using her flawless instincts to gauge his reaction. Soon enough, he's on his way back holding two beautiful ancient books and although both books stack up on his impossibly long arms, they seem like pocketbooks.

"OK, let's see. I have here the perfect conjure to drive away obsession and obfuscation. It's not as old as most of the books, scribbles, and scrolls I have in here, but its wisdom is timeless. Please allow me to read it to you.

"Snap"
(Snap Out of It)
There are moments in life that overwhelm us,

they seize us right at the gut level,

suddenly, we are crumbling inside,

without a clue,

how to cope with the situation.

Sometimes, it is simply doubt creeping in,

or anguish spreading throughout our spirit

or cold paralyzing fear.

Some others, the shell shock is much more profound,

as we might be in pain or grieving a loss.

But in modern life though,

the prevailing catalysts are,

pressure and stress,

induced by an ever-increasing overload,

coupled with a frantic and neurotic pace.

But, what about simply snapping out of it!

Snap!

Snap out of it!

Snap away from the moment,

freeze the picture around you,

freeze life's image,

just freeze it!
And separate yourself from the situation you are in.
Think only in nice, beautiful images
and let them take you over.
Focus on what you have, not on what you don't,
zero in on what you hold, not on what you lost,
then, dream about what you want,
visualizing yourself going for it, with all your heart.
Snap out of it without fear, do it without doubts,
remind yourself that quitting
does not exist in your vocabulary.
Snap away automatically,
right when the situation arises,
without delay, as you have to catch
these poisonous states before they start.
Now relax.
Let go.
Contemplate the image you've frozen
from the outside.
Then, as you decompress you'll realize
what your coping mechanisms are.
Did you focus on one thing and one thing only?
If so, then you snapped away
through a meditative state.
Or did you simply do it by being aware

of the situation and separating yourself from it?

Or did you do it by freezing the moment?

Freezing the image?

Freezing the picture?

Or did you do all of them?

In the end, how you did it, matters only,

as to the path to take next time.

What is really important,

is that now you know, how to snap out,

and how to snap away from the moment.

And you now know,

how to conquer life's circumstances,

before they conquer you.

As Mr. L finishes reading in the magnificent oak and mahogany store, Vicky stares intensely at Erasmus, looking for a reaction of acceptance and understanding. 'If he truly paid attention, this will help him,' she mulls over with her seemingly infallible instincts.

"It's not about snapping out and losing control, but exactly the opposite. It's about snapping out to regain control of yourself and the circumstances or situations you may be in." Mr. L correctly senses that the reading has had a major impact on Erasmus, who is fighting his own demons.

"Erasmus, think of it as a safety mechanism, an emergency brake that halts you right at the beginning, preventing anything from even getting started. The idea is that you catch yourself before you lose yourself into whatever world you are about to fall into, especially one where you are always your very own worst enemy."

"Fine, I get it, I get it," snaps Erasmus seemingly surrendering. "OK Vicky, I'll do it. Promise. I will."

"Victoria, I have a second poem. It's about uncluttered and dreamy spirits," announces Mr. Lafayette, eager to continue.

Mr. L then starts to read a scribble that begins on the rooftops of London:

"The Chimney Sweep"

The chimney sweep sits on the rooftops
of the city's moonless night.
Stars by the millions gaze at him,
like a magnificent gathering in the universe,
through luminescent eyes,
with infinite shades of white,
in full display, just for him.
The sweep is done for the night.
His job thoroughly completed,
having uncluttered and unplugged,
the chimneys and spirits,

of the city dwellers.

Now he waits for the spectacle to begin.

Then, as the large metropolis falls asleep,

with its gateways and launching pads ready,

free of any debris or impediments,

the city and its people are ready to start dreaming.

So it begins …

First a few,

then an avalanche of people's dreams,

fly unimpeded,

out of countless chimneys into the night sky.

They are like projectiles flying straight

into the firmament of the universe,

taking dreamers' dreams,

far away into the limitless space,

in the direction and watchful eyes,

of millions of stars waiting for them.

"We all need our chimney sweeps to free up our spirits, and dreams to fly far away and high up, into the deepest confines of the universe," states an inspired Mr. L. From that moment on, a beautiful bond grows between Mr. L and the young lovers. Although infrequent, every time the football team is even remotely close to New Heaven, they meet up. As predicted by Victoria, over time the relation between Mr. L and Erasmus becomes an intrinsical part of the future poet and professor's life - even after her vanishing act. And, Mr. Lafayette's wisdom becomes a guiding light through the years of Erasmus' solitude.

Royal Cambridge Scholastic Institute (2018)
(University's Auditorium)

Professor Cromwell-Smith brings his class back to the present. However, there are only a few looks that seem to show a preference for such a return.

"The memorable encounter with Mr. Lafayette not only dote us with a couple of invaluable life tools but also provided us with a crucial existential realization about our fallibility. Class, what happened to Vicky and I – the parting – could easily happen to you as well. So, in order to avoid it, pull yourself out and disengage from the situation by freezing it. Extracting yourself, snapping out of it, allows for the observation of facts from the outside and enables the day, circumstance, and road ahead of you, to be clear and free of your own persona, blocking it, perhaps even sabotaging all of it.

'They all want more,' he realizes and then adds some wisdom to conclude.

"In order for our dreams to soar unimpeded, we all need to make a deliberate effort to constantly cleanse our spirits," states the professor bringing the class to a close.

"Class, next week we are going to travel back to the moment when Vicky and I met a very special person who lived in the outskirts of Boston. A person who touched our lives forever."

Then as the professor leaves, his students' faces seem to reflect that they are either trying to "snap out" or "getting ready" to fly away as the dreams of dreamers do.

CHAPTER 5

FAITH

Royal Cambridge Scholastic Institute (2018)
(Erasmus and Victoria's Campus Home)

It is early morning, near dawn when Erasmus suddenly awakens.

"What is it dear?" asks Victoria.

Erasmus is drenched in sweat and his eyes are glossy and disoriented. Slowly he comes to and recognizes in comfort, that she's lying next to him.

"I was having a bad dream," he replies still half asleep.

Victoria flashes concern followed by determination.

"The same dream?"

"Yes," he replies in frustration and impotence.

"Look at me!" she says holding his face with both her hands.

"I'm not going anywhere my love. Erasmus you've got to have faith," she says with conviction as he nods in embarrassment, snapping out of it.

(Campus Backroads)

Not long after, giggling and laughing, they pedal through the mildly cold autumn weather zigzagging down the streets with a lazy cadence, seemingly as if nothing happened.

"Faith, Erasmus. I never lost faith that I would find you somewhere further down the road of life," she states assertively.

Then as the enamored couple approaches the main faculty building, Erasmus has another illumination. "Do you remember when we both ran into Faith?" asks an inspired Erasmus.

"You mean Thomas Albert Faith?" asks Victoria in delight.

Ever so slightly, Erasmus nods with a mischievous affirmation.

"Of course I do," replies Victoria.

"Dear, your class better be prepared for it. What a magnificent idea! Just be yourself," she states giving Erasmus that little extra boost that he has become accustomed to.

Royal Cambridge Scholastic Institute (2018)
(University's Auditorium)

The class is all assembled and ready when Professor Cromwell-Smith storms in full of energy.

"Hello class."

"Hello professor," reply quite a few of them.

"Today, you'll meet a very special man that changed both Vicky's and my outlook on life, something that I desperately needed in order to grow stronger spiritually and emotionally. It begins like this ..."

Riverside Village on the Boston Suburbs (1976)

Victoria and Erasmus have been rowing for hours on the Charles River. Their cadence and rhythm are slow and steady. Their rowboat is uncomfortably narrow but thrillingly fast. The young couple is synchronized to choreographic perfection in fitness and strokes. Along the way, they stop a few times. First, they stop to have lunch at a seafood joint right by the river's edge. In rowing clothes and all, they enter in pressing hunger.

"I love all of the colored ribbons weaved through your hair," he says gallantly.

She smiles mischievously.

"And I would like to switch places when we go back to rowing," she replies in jest.

"What?" asks a puzzled Erasmus.

"Let me be the one that gets to see your gorgeous silhouette in the foreground of the scenery, on the way home."

In return, Erasmus flashes a big smile for his vivacious muse.

"So, your first ever New England clam chowder was in Boston?" she teases him as he gulps chunks of the famous local dish.

"Yes," Erasmus replies gulping even faster.

Their second stop is at a lovely glass-enclosed riverside winter garden that catches their attention not only because of the oddity of its location but also because of its magnificent and lush colors.

Inside, the garden is even prettier with winding labyrinthic paths. Then, as they make a turn on a corner impregnated with flowers, they see a man reading what appears to be a mammoth book. The book lies on a picnic table and the reader sits right across from it on a wooden bench. The pair of youngsters stop right in their tracks. The gold burnished pages and old leather-bound immediately catch Erasmus' attention.

"That's a very old book," he observes. "I wonder why he would have it here in the open, seldom if ever one sees that."

The man, on the other hand, is so absorbed as he reads that at first, he does not notice them. Without hesitation, Erasmus walks in his direction. The sound of the pebble steps is noticed. The burly man with light brown hair comes out of his trance and briefly glances at them. He stands up with the voluminous book as if cradling it, with both arms extended forward, and leaves in a hurry.

Erasmus and Vicky follow in tandem from a distance. After they walk through the narrow streets of the small village on the outskirts of Boston, they see the burly man entering a store.

"Let's wait here and see what happens," states Erasmus.

Just a few minutes after, the man leaves and briefly glances at them before marching away. The book is no longer in his possession. Tentatively, they approach the store. They're in for a big surprise. As they get closer they see a sign that reads: "Faith Antique Books & Co. (est. 1907)."

A smaller sign further down the display window reads: "Please inquire about a limited number of our books available to let."

'That explains it,' reasons Erasmus, remembering the burly man carrying the book to the store.

"Erasmus, do you think there are only religious books in there?" asks Victoria as they approach the store.

"It may well be that, but faith isn't just a religious term."

He opens the door hesitantly. The bell announcing them reminds him of his childhood years roaming through his hometown's countless antique book stores that had the same sounds, scents, and layouts. The store is nothing like they expected. It is stark and modern, built out of chrome and glass. There are ten rows with long hallways starting right at the entrance. The ceiling is perhaps thirty feet high and chrome and glass bookshelves reach all the way up.

"I have been around this neck of the woods for thirty years and this is a first for me," states a bold stocky man with a high-pitched voice and a solemn but amused face.

Startled and puzzled by his remark, Vicky and Erasmus are caught off guard and turn rather brusquely to face the voice coming at them.

"I mean coming to visit us dressed in oarsmen clothes."

The youngsters both laugh and release whatever tension there was in the air. Now it is their turn.

"This is also the first of its kind that I've ever been to," states Erasmus assertively.

"How so?" their host inquires intrigued.

"A faith-focused antique bookstore," states a loquacious Erasmus.

Now it's the store owner that laughs hard, loud, and long. Erasmus and Vicky learn that the store owner is a Harvard business school graduate and worked for a while as an investment banker for a large Wall Street firm. The bank stationed him in London for over a decade. That's where he met and married his second wife, an antiquarian that introduced him to what became his passion – the world of antique books. Eventually, he abandoned the world of finance altogether.

"Faith is my name, I am Thomas Albert Faith. We carry books of many kinds and from all sorts of life."

"I am Erasmus Cromwell-Smith."

"I am Victoria Emerson-Lloyd."

"I gather you two have a knack for the kind of treasures we hold in here."

"Indeed we do sir. Indeed we do."

"Call me Mr. Faith please. Now, how can I be of service to you? I have to presume it'll include shipping, due to the absence of dryness on your means of transportation."

'I love how he talks. He is direct, warm and at least now, is genuinely placing us at the center of his universe. I really like him. I'll bet that he and Erasmus will have a lasting relationship as well,' Vicky reflects putting to good use once more, her impeccable instincts.

"Actually, Mr. Faith, we were wondering if you could share with us some of your scribbles on a particular subject matter?" asks an inquisitive Erasmus.

"And what would that be?"

"He struggles with it all the time!" interrupts Vicky, as the opportunity presents itself to deal with lingering issues.

Erasmus leans back with an expression of surrender. Besides, he's in for the experience of entering the world of ancient writing, period. The subject covered isn't so important as long as the store master is the guide. So, he erroneously thinks.

"And what does he struggle with?"

"You'll find it amusing and without question soaked, as we are, with serendipity."

The brief pause that ensues is filled with mystery as Vicky stares intensely at the storekeeper.

"Faith," she finally says.

"Yes?" inquires Mr. F.

"No, Faith," insists Vicky continuing the ruse.

"What?" asks a confused Mr. F.

"The subject he struggles with, all of the time is faith. Would you have an impactful old writing that could bring some modicum of existential clarity to my disbelieving partner? Would you, or is the only faith in here, you?" she pleads in joyful expectation to Erasmus' regretful realization.

Mr. Faith smiles with tight lips with a "you've got me" expression of amusement and pleasure.

"I will share with the two of you something I've treasured all my adult life."

Mr. F walks in little bouncy side steps, down the second hallway of the store. He stops midway and goes up a ladder until, about twenty feet up; he pulls out a relatively small blue-colored book and waves it in the air. Soon enough, Mr. Faith is sitting with them on a small chrome and glass round table. He then starts to read in earnest.

"Faith"

Faith is a celestial force that we willfully invoke,

to profess our credos with overwhelming intensity.

Faith morphs <u>believing</u> into an unstoppable inner strength that

becomes our spiritual engine and dotes on us with a

continuum of goodness

and a giving soul.

Faith is awareness of the spirit

with mindfulness of the soul.

Faith is the indispensable source

of meaning in our lives.

Faith is mysterious as it deals with two rational unsolvable and

existential questions:

the conundrum of creation a

and the enigma of a higher calling.

Faith is the realization that even though there are many questions about our universe's origin, that we don't have an answer for - neither do we have proof about how it was created nor do we know where we are going after life - we still deliberately chose to believe wholeheartedly and steadfastly in the existence of a creator of it all.

Faith is unconditional love, as well as, the immutable, unstoppable, unwavering, unflickering, stubborn, and indomitable belief that there is a reason and a purpose for us being here

- dictated by our creator.

When we profess it inside of a cocoon, faith is nothing but an empty shell of falsehood. Individualistic faith thrives behind shields and walls of weakness, erected to shy away from the world through pitiful, self-serving beliefs that are just tunnel vision fantasies of our mind,

like mirages in the desert.

The world of darkness awaits us when faith is blind. A life without a periscope may lead us into perilous paths filled with dire and unintended consequences.

When faith is misguided, life quickly loses its compass and purpose.

Life becomes rudderless and without direction –
we are propelled forward by fake passions and beliefs, into tumbling trajectories, where, if our endeavors prove to be

hazardous or hurtful, faith becomes a runaway train that

inexorably derails, crashes,

and burns.

To the contrary, faith is authentic when driven by virtue,

the creator, or both.

But, we are not born in faith or virtue as both have to be

acquired and they grow in tandem,

feeding off each other.

Faith in particular ages over time, like a good wine, out of our

relentless pursuit, through hard work and discipline, of virtue,

excellence, and an inalterable and unassailable belief in the

creator of all things.

When we have faith,

We see light in darkness,

We give love when there is hate,

We offer compassion when there is

suffering and pain,

We provide healing when there are wounds,

We show loyalty when there is betrayal,

We eagerly reconcile when there is conflict,

We readily forgive when there is hurt,

We sacrifice and abnegate

for those that need it most,

We ascent and rise to the occasion when the situation could

not be worse,

We acquiesce and adjourn

when the circumstances require it,

We are always austere and humble,

We are grateful and anonymous in our actions,

and our heart is pure, crystalline,

joyful, and wholesome.

Above all, we blindly trust what our creator teaches and

expects of us.

When we have faith we acclaim life and humanity,

elevating our existence to a higher calling, one where we

acquire through creed and conversion, a noble purpose of

spirit and a God-driven meaning for the soul.

As Mr. F finishes, the written and powerful words linger in the air and throughout the store.

"Young man, use faith as a source of inner strength, it'll teach you not only to believe but also to see through any obstacles life may present to you. Faith also is the best resource to neutralize and overcome doubt, indecisiveness, and especially fear. Erasmus, the more faith you profess, the more you grow as a man."

Royal Cambridge Scholastic Institute (2018)
(University Auditorium)

Professor Cromwell-Smith reluctantly brings back his audience, "class, faith is the strongest, deepest, most indomitable and unbreakable of all beliefs. It'll carry you through the most profound of all sorrows and pain; through devastating losses and seasons of weakness; through obliterating storms and shattering quakes. Faith enables all of you, to forgive with grace and give without expecting rewards or gratitude. Faith dotes on you with a benevolent heart, a driven spirit, a calm, kindred and meaningful soul. Faith is always pure and genuine, as we profess it, walking alongside the creator." The oratory now concluded, he allows time for questions.

"Professor Cromwell-Smith, isn't faith a religious term then?" a tall, pale bespectacled young woman asks.

"Religion is the most commonly known method, not the only one though, of how to practice faith in life. We profess faith in our partner, our loved ones, humanity, our friends, among others," replies the professor.

"So, faith is not exclusive to any particular religion?" asks the same student.

"No, it isn't, as it's practiced by all religions. Faith is the driving force behind all of them. Faith lies inside, ready to be lit and provide us with a celestial halo that glows outside but comes from within. We all breathe earth's air in the same way in spite of our differences. In final analysis, a good analogy to think of is that although we do it from different parts of our planet, we all breathe the very same air."

"I'll see you all next week."

But, as he leaves he is deeply moved by the facial expressions of the attendees as he realizes that they are all wearing expressions of hope, which is an existential condition of faith.

CHAPTER 6

LIFE, EVOLUTION AND CHANGE

Royal Cambridge Scholastic Institute (2018)
(Erasmus and Victoria's Campus Home)

The smell wakes her up. A breakfast basket of French pastries and croissants sits on her bed.

'How does he do it again and again?' Vicky blurts, still half-asleep, as she stretches. A tune plays softly in the background. Jimmy Durante's "Make Someone Happy," one of her favorite tunes, has her inhaling deep, as she soon finds herself once again starting the day happy and smiling thanks to her beloved Brit.

'Every day and every moment counts,' she reminds herself while following Erasmus' existential credo.

'Live each day as if it is your last,' she dutifully recites while getting up, and shortly after wanders around the house in search of her other half. When she finds him, after her exuberant and effusive giggles, followed by hugs and kisses, they sit down to eat.

"It still baffles me that, for years we went to some of the same antiquarians right here in the city and never ran into each other," Victoria whispers while sipping her morning tea and munching her much-beloved Gallic treats.

"Even more puzzling is the fact that knowing us both, Mr. Ringwald never put us in contact," laments Erasmus in vain.

"Out of prudence and discretion dear, he knew about my marriage and kids. He also knew about your pain and despair," Vicky reflects with caution.

"Vic, was he right though? I don't know for certain."

"Yes, he was. For example, did you ever inquire specifically about me or my whereabouts?" she asks him.

"No, I didn't. It never occurred to me," replies Erasmus in submissive realization.

"Well, neither did I. Maybe there was a part of me then that did not want to know. I guess the more rational and sensical side of me that recognized that I had a family and a husband that came first, just didn't want to go there," she states trying, unconvincingly, to justify herself.

"Our affinity for antique bookstores, while in solitude, was a way to keep a faint link between us," Erasmus wonders.

"Perhaps, that's what it was," she confirms still unconvinced as she hands the car keys to Erasmus.

As they walk out, the cold air is immediately omnipresent. The morning's landscape is white and frosty as, after a major snowstorm the night before, winter has officially made itself present in New England.

"Vic, today's class will be about the memorable day we met Mr. R for the first time," states Erasmus.

"Mr. R, how can I forget the little great man? That day we met him is one that I've treasured my entire life," says Victoria totally lost in sweet memories of the past.

"Everything about that encounter was so special," she says with glittering eyes.

"Tell you what my irresistible Brit; I am coming with you today. How much time have we got?" she states and quizzes matter of fact, to Erasmus' total surprise.

"About 45 minutes to the beginning of the class," he replies.

"I still need to make a quick stop at BU beforehand," Victoria announces.

"Whatever my lady may require, I'm glad to oblige," Erasmus answers in bliss.

Fittingly, the hurried ride acquires a feminine touch as Victoria applies a bit of makeup, something he loves watching her do, as they drive along the frozen landscape towards her university. Not long after, still excited at the prospect of her attending his class, Erasmus pulls into Vicky's BU faculty building driveway.

"I will just sign a couple of things and inform them that I will be arriving by the end of the morning. I will only be about 10 minutes," she says while quickly exiting the car.

"Careful with the ice Vic," Erasmus yells from the window, but she is already gone.

Royal Cambridge Scholastic Institute (2018)
(University Auditorium)

Forty-five minutes later and right on the dot, the professor and his beloved one, stroll into class. Victoria walks straight into the students sitting area, but before she takes a seat, the audience reacts and starts clapping and cheering in delight. Only the professor clearing his throat stops the warm welcome. The entire auditorium is filled with good energy and excitement. Seemingly, the collective thought is that there has to be a very good reason for her to be in the class, on this particular day.

"Good morning everyone," states the professor with a broad smile.

"Good morning," is the collective teasing reply, as many still recall the last time they saw Victoria the previous semester, on the memorable day of her reencounter with the professor.

"Well as you have all noticed, we have a special self-invited guest this morning," the professor announces still in bliss.

"I can assure you that I was as surprised as you all were when I learned about her impromptu visit with us today," states the professor to a captivated audience, that is not only not missing a single word, but collectively keeps on glancing at a now quite embarrassed Victoria.

"The fact is, when my other half learned about what I would be talking about this morning, she didn't want to miss it for the world," the professor proudly announces.

"Well, with all of that being said, the story begins like this…"

Harvard Theatre (1976)

Erasmus is peeking at the audience through the curtains, but can't find her. All of the careful planning will be for nothing if she's not present.

'Something happened, I'm sure about it,' young Erasmus thinks in near despair. Most of the audience is already seated. 'Where is she?' he asks in a panic.

"The event is about to begin. Everyone, please take a seat," says the public announcer.

'Should I quit?' asks Erasmus in doubt.

'This was not a good idea, you've never done this in front of an audience,' quibbles Erasmus all by himself.

"Good morning everyone. Welcome to the 10ᵗʰ Annual Poetry Contest. Let me introduce you to the jury," states the host of the event.

'Point of no return mate. You can't back out now. In a few minutes, you'll have to walk the plank while making a complete fool out of yourself,' Erasmus laments in defeated abandonment.

He peeks through the curtains one last time and sees her sitting in the front row. While preoccupied with his panicky state, he totally missed her arrival. His excitement and adrenaline quickly take over and his whole self starts to get back to his plan for the day. He looks again and this time smiles within himself. Confidence is back. He is ready.

The two close friends are attending a poetry contest for the first time. Victoria seems at ease – perhaps a tad sad. Gina on the other hand seems out of place and a bit surprised.

"Where is Erasmus?" asks Vicky's best friend Gina.

"Couldn't make it, but he pleaded with me not to miss it, so I can tell him everything about it later tonight," replies Vicky still feeling empty inside because of his absence.

At that moment, Erasmus' thoughts are interrupted by the master of ceremonies.

"Our first contestant comes from Wales, Great Britain. His name is Erasmus Cromwell-Smith and he will be reading a very special poem, dedicated to an unwitting but much-beloved person in the audience, Mrs. Victoria Emerson-Lloyd – could you please stand?"

Vicky is not only completely caught off guard, but she is also choked up with emotion as she stands. She has a knot in her throat and feels like she is suffocating. But as Erasmus walks onto the podium with his loving eyes fixated on her, she looks at him in return and her whole body relaxes, and a broad smile forms. Then, Erasmus starts to read and his words immediately enrapture her.

"Whispering at Your Heart"

What is it that is so magnificent about you?

You are special because you are

unique and inimitable,

You are magical because everything you touch with your

magic wand,

falls under a divine incantation,

You are beautiful as your heart is,

You are intense as your feelings are,

You are as driven and indomitable

as your passions are,

You are as immutably firm as you are fiercely loyal,

You are made out of unwavering convictions and unbreakable

beliefs,

You are tirelessly steady because of your relentless discipline

and perseverance because your consistency never waivers or

ceases to be,

You are sincere, genuine, and honest

because irrespective of what others think or say,

you always follow your heart.

You are built out of unlimited strength,

courage, and integrity,

You are so valiant, that again and again,

you always defeat fear,

You are pretty in the morning

and even prettier at sundown,

You are genuine and adorable because you are filled

with innocence and candor,

You are noble and dependable,

because rain or shine, wind or heavy seas,

you are always there,

You are virtuous and giving

because you are always ready

to forgive and help others,

You are humble,

as you are quick to admit your faults,

and make amends at lightning speed,

And you have this eternal halo,

made by heaven's angels,

which dotes you with this impenetrable shield

that protects you against anything or anyone,

as it is built out of unshakable faith,

a steadfast character,

a wholesome set of virtues, and a fierce and relentless pursuit

of excellence.

All of this and much more is you, Vicky,

You are my life's journey companion,

You are my true love,

I love you,

Forever yours, Erasmus.

As the applause and cheers rise, they look into each other's eyes. The enamored twosome generates such an intense vibe between them, the place, audience, and jurors disappear. All of a sudden, it is only the two of them standing alone in their own wonderful world.

"Thank you," she whispers with her lips as both hands are bundled around her heart.

He tips his head in acknowledgment while his own hands imitate hers.

Then the self-absorbed duo simply stares at each other in infatuation for a brief moment that feels eternal in intensity.

The Streets of Downtown Boston (1976)

When the young poet comes out from backstage and sits next to his other half, the couple in love, just want to be alone. So, they decide to go for a stroll and leave the theatre. Soon, they are wandering around, walking and chatting endlessly, laughing, enjoying their age, and why not, being foolish as well. The noise of downtown Boston brings them back to an unwelcome but omnipresent reality. Then, as the sounds of the city try to pierce their bubble, Erasmus steers them both into the direction of the river's shore. As they cross a dead-end street something catches Erasmus's eye. It's just a quick and passing glance, but it's enough to trigger his "adaptive subconscious," and in a split second he turns around. His instincts are quickly validated. A cart being pulled at the street's end is carrying a bunch of voluminous books. Victoria sees the look on his face and follows his penetrating eyes. Her spontaneous reaction shows that she's not only as surprised as him but has learned her lesson and knows that she should trust and follow his literary impulses. "Are those what I think they are?" she asks in awe and wonder. "Indeed they are Vic, let's go and check them out."

While holding hands, the twosome walks briskly in the direction of the books. As they approach a building, they stop right in their tracks.

"Ringwald and Brothers Antiquarians (est. 1860)."

In the window are two big round stickers: "Going out for business sale."

In the meantime, the cart they saw earlier has been dropped at the store's entrance. That's when they see a diminutive man, perhaps 5'2" to 5'3" tall walking outside to the cart and carrying books inside. He looks eccentric if a bit odd, wearing a reddish plaid vest, and exhibiting arms, head, and shoes that are way too big for his height. Born in Boston, Perceval Ringwald married late – in his mid-forties – 25 happily ever after years ago. He kept the promise he made to his fellow antiquarian wife on their wedding night to take her to every place in the world he had been to before they met. So, that's what they do and continue to do, travel the world when not immersed in their own passions, namely philosophy, poetry, and his antique bookstore.

Vicky and Erasmus see him unload the books in a whisper, literally displaying the strength of an ant. When he is done, he comes back outside, pulls the cart to one side, and unexpectedly turns around facing them with his hands on his hips.

"What are the two of you waiting for?" the spec of a man suddenly asks the jolted duo.

Victoria and Erasmus tighten their handhold, but as they remain speechless trying to figure out how to respond, he surprises them even more. "Erasmus and Victoria right?" he quizzes with a mischievous face.

Now the two youngsters look at each other in disbelief.

"What did you expect? The two of you have been making noise around a very small community." He continues, as his friendly stare relaxes them a bit.

"Good noise, I shall say. A very good one indeed." His statement makes them feel totally relaxed.

As they walk in, the place immediately impacts them. The layout of the store is stunning with mahogany from the floor up to a thirty-foot ceiling in a big rectangle. There are no hallways. The whole place is all in front of them with thousands upon thousands of perfectly lined books, thirty feet high.

"How come you are going out of business?" asks a puzzled and perturbed Erasmus while contemplating the magnificent athenaeum."

"When have you seen products being carted into a going out of business store?" the spirited store manager replies with a question.

"I guess never sir," answers a very confused Erasmus.

"Exactly, and what does that mean then?" the store owner states, still not providing an answer.

"Is it just a marketing ploy then?" Vicky asks with ingenuity and hesitation.

"Right on Victoria, right on. The key lies in the word "for" instead of "of", continues the diminutive man, finally providing a reply.

"Sir, you know our names but we don't know yours," affirms Vicky with confidence.

"You think you don't, but you do, or what else could it be?" he replies again with another question.

'His replies come only if one figures out the answers to the questions. Riddler, that's how I'm going to call him, Mr. R a/k/a the Riddler. That's it,' thinks Victoria, her natural instincts in full motion.

"OK Mr. R we get it, we get it," replies Erasmus as if reading half of Vicky's mind.

"So, I'm Mr. R and that's my forever moniker, I presume?" asks an amused but pleased Mr. Ringwald.

'I'll bet anything that Mr. R will become Erasmus' mentor in adulthood,' she guesses with a strong gut feeling about it.

Erasmus walks around the wooden wonder with hands on his back. He looks at everything around him in detail and doesn't miss a thing.

"Mr. R what about change?" asks Erasmus, in his typical self-absorbed and nerdy fashion.

"What about it?" the Riddler asks back.

"Would you have something about that subject?"

"Why are you interested in such a theme-like change?"

"Erasmus has difficulty with change Mr. R. Change does not come easy to him," interjects Victoria with exacting perception.

"What about evolution?" replies the inveterate riddling inquisitor from downtown Boston.

"Are you recommending we read about evolution instead?" asks Erasmus, starting to get the hang of his incessant questions, and liking it more and more by the moment.

"Not instead of, but together. Don't you know that change and evolution are tightly coupled together as if joined at the hip?" Mr. R replies.

He moves quickly around using small steps. With a small portable hi-lo pushed up to the store's right side wall, he goes up and stops at the halfway point. He then picks up a massive volume from one of the shelves.

"Victoria and Erasmus, this scribble is about change and evolution, through a prism of philosophical prose," he announces as he returns. "Let me read it to both of you," the Riddler states as he begins to read in earnest.

"Life, Evolution and Change Among Us"

Two of the most fundamental
and existential states in life
are measured by each stroke forward
in our life clock's hands.
The corroboratory tick of the larger and faster one
is that of <u>the sound of change</u>,
and the smaller and slower one,
validating clicks are those of <u>the sound of</u> <u>evolution</u>.
If the minutes tick,
then the hours will inevitably click as well.
Change engenders evolution,
not the other way around.
If change is the transition
from one condition to another,
Then evolution is a series
of guided changes of advancement.
Change is doors opening,
Evolution takes and keeps us inside.
Change is the pursuit of something new, different, and
perhaps disrupting.
Evolution is the realization of such an endeavor.

Change is the end of a paradigm,

evolution is the new one.

Change requires willingness and desire,

evolution is self-evident.

Change could trigger second chances;

evolution is the second chance itself.

Change is lasting and most effective

when accompanied by

Consciousness and rewarded by evolution.

When change is humble, real change inside is likely and we

evolve.

Change and dogma as a rigid set of beliefs

are like oil and water.

Evolution is the filter that separates

and discards dogma away.

Change is easily measurable in magnitudes;

it is seasonal and occurs in batches.

Evolution is easily quantifiable as well.

It is constant and transits through all seasons.

When we change for others, our heart is king

and evolution is our new and richer royal heart.

When circumstances or others change us,

the existence or lack of evolution

is the incontrovertible evidence on whether change

is for better or worse.

Change is fruitful when driven by mindfulness;

evolution is the fruit of such behavior.

Real change requires truthfulness;

evolution is the validation of such platitude.

Monsters could be born out of change

when combined with material things

such as greed or power;

then, instead of evolution,

we could regress backward on a downward spiral.

Change could also be opportunistic

and circumstantial

or it could be rehearsed and deliberate,

but its execution and validation

are essentially the same,

the old trusty tool of evolution.

When we change, we willingly want to transfer, break, pass

over, disrobe, mutate, alter, modify, transform, convert, vary,

substitute, exchange, replace, switch a position or course,

status or state, depart from beliefs, credos or norms;

deviate from character, sequence or condition; insurge, diverge

or shift.

But, it is only through evolution

that we execute them all.

Change is not constrained by time,

but by opportune circumstances.

Evolution is the reward for proper timing.

Change is virtuous when driven by moral truisms

and the choice of excellence;

evolution is the actual acquisition of such virtues.

Change is observed, recognized, and valued when not self-

proclaimed or bragged about,

and the proof of such worthy behavior

lies in the presence or absence of evolution

as a consequence of our behavior.

As we are afraid of it,

change requires courage and valor;

then, the resulting evolution is our medal of honor.

Through change and evolution, our life is never still,

always moving forward,

constantly renewing itself in a state of constant flux.

If we embrace change, we are in harmony

and in accordance with the laws of nature

and the rules of life,

welcoming one of our universal key dimensions,

that of perennial and endless transformation,

where the sounds of change

and the winds of evolution,

tick and click in sync,

inexorably forward and never swaying away.

"Victoria and Erasmus, I believe it was Machiavelli who stated: "If you want to see people at their worst, bring them changes." Our fear of change makes us build roadblocks and excuses on our existential paths, based on false perceptions of comfort, safety, and what we are used to. But, these are simply artificial obstacles we can wipe out in an instant, as change is always and only one will away," states Mr. Ringwald.

Royal Cambridge Scholastic Institute (2018)
(University Auditorium)

In front of the startled looks of his student body, Professor Cromwell-Smith comes back to reality with dreamy eyes. "A great deal of the art of a wholesome life, resides in the power of change, by constantly renewing and reinventing oneself. Don't be afraid of it," Cromwell professes as he smiles in satisfaction to his audience.

He pans across the room as if trying to connect with each one of his students. Then, he focuses on Victoria. She's standing with tears in her eyes and a huge smile on her face. Once more, as forty years earlier, with both hands on her heart, she whispers at him in a slow, deliberate voice "THANK YOU."

Again, he in turn slightly tips his head in acknowledgment, while he brings both hands on top of his heart and whispers with a mime's lips to her "I LOVE YOU."

The student body is in total awe as their beloved professor and his soul mate are in a trance as if frozen in time in their own private world.

Professor Cromwell-Smith walks out holding hands with Victoria to a delighted audience. In many of his students, the pedagogue can see a twinkle in their eyes – one of openness to change and a resolute belief to evolve as well.

CHAPTER 7

LIFE WIZARDS

Royal Cambridge Scholastic Institute (2018)
(Erasmus and Victoria's Campus Home)

It's an old habit, Erasmus always waking up earlier than Victoria. It's usually still dark when he starts roaming around the house, something he seldom did when living alone. And this isn't the only routine they have seemingly reacquired from their life together as youngsters. In several ways, it doesn't feel like they were apart from each other for so many years. Fittingly, today Erasmus is about to find out that life around him is even rosier than his idealist spirit makes him believe. It happens as he enters his studio and turns the brass floor lamp on. The gleam from the golden burnished letters immediately grabs his full attention. Lying on one of his old trusted Chesterfield reading sofas is an antique book that he has searched for his entire life. With his emotions soaring and his mind shut down, he lifts the precious old book.

'Life Wizards,' the title reads.

"I've looked for you, for so long." Erasmus rejoices as he talks to the book in a whisper.

'Where did you come from?' Erasmus asks himself. 'Who found you?'

As he opens the book, a card inside falls to the floor.

'Who else but my lady,' he realizes, recognizing her handwriting at once.

Book in hand, he takes a seat on his beloved reading sofa and starts to read in earnest.

"You make me so happy Erasmus. How could I have left you? How could I have deserted us? Please forgive me. I know that you've wanted to possess this book ever since the days you first read it with your childhood mentor, Mrs. V. I've never forgotten the day you read those wonderful passages and essays to me. That was the day we stumbled onto the book at the Library of Congress. With all my love. Yours forever, Victoria."

Erasmus becomes teary-eyed and lost in his own thoughts. Then, he sees her standing by the door.

"Oh Vic, you shouldn't have. This must have cost you a fortune. How did you find it?" he says in a flurry of words while holding her tight against him.

She looks at him straight in the eye with a deadly serious stare.

"I am sorry," she says.

"Sorry about what?"

"I made a terrible mistake back then."

"But you were forced to."

"That's the sanitized version for my children."

"What are you talking about?"

"No adult can be forced to marry in our country, at least not where I come from," she affirms in sleepy whispers.

Erasmus pauses at the realization. He instinctively lets her continue without a word and is quickly rewarded with a torrent of words soaked in repressed guilt.

"Even though I never admitted it, reality was that part of me was intimidated by your intellect and your knowledge. I saw you grow every day, and week after week, I felt as if I was falling more and more behind. Sometimes, I would tell Gina that I was afraid of you, but what I really was afraid of was you leaving me behind. Erasmus, I was not raised to play second fiddle to a profoundly gifted individual. I was supposed to shine and be the star of the show. Since my early years as an only child, I was the center of attention and affection for my entire family. Then at school, in sports, or anything competitive, I was the best. Then I met you," she says crying on his shoulder.

In between sobs, she manages to continue, letting it all out, while Erasmus just listens, stunned by her outburst, but not surprised by her words.

"The fact is that I felt inadequate. So, I started building this silent resentment and anger towards you. It was something I couldn't control or manage, as it comingled every day with the love I felt for you. A battle started brewing inside of me like Oscar Wild describes in his book, The Picture of Dorian Grey. I was splitting into two personalities, good and evil. As its manifestations began to grow, I would make, hidden in satire, off-the-cuff sarcastic remarks about you to our common friends, or I would interrupt or cut you off each time you spoke in front of others. Then, with the antiquarians, I started to direct the readings to flaws that I would verbalize about you. Over time, I started building up a number of reasons why I couldn't stay with you. At the same time, stupidly, I would go on and on, over a growing laundry list of things I was better at than you. Throughout all of this, in your wonderful absentmindedness world, you perennially trivialized the mundane versus the sacred things. You were totally and utterly oblivious to all the turbulence and storms building inside of me, and that drove me even crazier. Bottom line Erasmus, my fears and insecurities were eating me up inside. So, when my parents, essentially my mother, presented their case for me to marry who they preferred over you, I let myself be persuaded. This gave me the perfect excuse and escape route. So, I jumped ship. By doing so, I betrayed my heart. I betrayed us and was disloyal to you. I made a terrible existential mistake. As happy as I find myself now and as happy as I feel you are as well, I have this enormous sense of guilt that's eating me up inside and won't go away. Day and night, I have this voice inside of me that repeats itself again and again with the same message: 'You don't deserve him.'"

Erasmus looks at her for a long time. To him, most of what she's just dumped is factually new, but not unexpected, as he always sensed there was more behind her sudden departure. Besides, he was always aware of her insecurities and blamed himself afterward for trivializing and not helping her to overcome them. 'What she didn't understand then, hopefully, she does now, is that I love her the way she is.'

"Vic, despite what you have just said, which all belongs to the past and no longer exists, I've never stopped loving you. That's what matters the most," Erasmus responds with profound wisdom, gallantry, and restraint as an overture to put things to rest and leave that long and painful chapter of their lives behind. "I have nothing to forgive you for. Your actions in the past are entirely yours, not mine. They affect you. They're your burden and yours alone. When what you do in life affects sacred matters as opposed to mundane ones, the first person you are accountable to is you. Therefore, the question is, have you forgiven yourself? If not, are you willing and capable of doing so? Because, in order to be happy while in love, you must be able to forgive not only others but yourself as well."

"But I've changed; I am not the same Erasmus."

"Let me be the judge of that Vicky. I can tell you that you haven't changed – not one bit. If anything, you've grown a great deal through the hardship you've experienced. Otherwise, you and your capacities and abilities to love and be loved are still the same."

"Why did you wait for me for so long?"

"For the same reasons that you did, neither of us found true love again."

"You never thought about it?" she asks.

"You don't think about those things Vicky. You either feel them or you don't."

"You know me well. There's nothing in the world that would persuade me to be with someone if I didn't love that person," he continues.

"When you truly love somebody, there is this magnificent state of mutual emotional dependence that is at the same time magical and extraordinarily beautiful. Once it is broken through, it is like delicate porcelain or fine crystal shattering into thousands of pieces that can't be put back together the same way, ever again. From then on, the best you can aspire to is to treasure a life and a person that no longer exists," Erasmus adds.

"Why did our porcelain, our crystal never break?" Victoria asks.

"I don't know exactly, but I guess in a way the bond itself never broke, and the loyalty and belief in each other never wavered. In final analysis and in matters of the heart, everything is driven by the strength and solidity of true love and the columns and foundations that sustain it," states Erasmus and to his great relief, he realizes her eyes are calm as if, once and for all, she finally feels unburdened.

By the time Professor Cromwell-Smith pedals his way to class, except for the precious and beloved book Victoria gave him, he has already blocked out everything about the last two enlightening hours with Vicky.

Royal Cambridge Scholastic Institute (2018)
(University Auditorium)

"Good morning, how's everyone today?"

"Insanely awesome, professor," replies a spirited class, to a grateful professor, who nods while showing a big broad smile. He then commences the class in earnest.

"Earlier this morning, Victoria presented this wonderful gift to me," states the professor while displaying it for everyone to see. "The book is called "Life Wizards." I first had the privilege of reading it at Mrs. V's place, who as you know was my trusted cheerleader and mentor back in Wales for the better part of my early life. After my beloved tutor passed away, I tried to acquire this book, but never could. Today I am going to take you back to a moment in time when the book was on loan to our Library of Congress. During that period, Vicky and I were visiting D.C. and ran into it by accident. It begins like this …"

Library of Congress, Washington, DC (1976)

The two youngsters are looking every which way. Now they gaze sideways and as they pan the magnificent library, their eyes

141

become fixed on each other and they burst into loud and strident laughter, which is not well received by others.

"This place is amazing," Victoria states.

"Alexandria, in ancient Egypt, has always been considered the biggest and richest library in regard to ancient history. This athenaeum, Vicky, is the Alexandria of modern history."

In town for a football road game, Erasmus and Victoria had planned their itinerary well in advance. Otherwise, it's hard to imagine where young Erasmus might have gone on his first ever visit to the nation's capital other than the greatest library on planet Earth. Excited as children and holding hands tightly, Erasmus leads her to the antique books section. Most of it is off-limits, so Erasmus decides to observe the most valuable old books from afar just to admire the art, materials, and front of their covers. Later, when they're about to leave, they walk over to the antique books open section. Erasmus focuses his attention on a series of books from a German author that one of his mentors, Mr. M, loved to read from. Then he sees it. His eyes widen and his neck stiffens and elongates like a wolf eyeing his prey. Vicky notices the reaction and immediately knows that he's seen something that he obsesses about.

"Vicky, that's the book I've talked so much about to you," he states while barely able to contain his enthusiasm.

"Which one?"

"Life Wizards," he states while guiding her over to the book.

"How did it make it here?" he wonders aloud.

A while later as they sit on a specially designated section to read it, they learn that the book is on loan from Mrs. V's "Sutton-Raleigh's Antique Books for the Young," store in Wales.

"My favorite poem from this book is "Life is Bliss" but there is also another great verse — my second favorite. It's about very special inspired people and how to spot them in life," states Erasmus as he selects the poem from the book.

"Let me read it to you," Erasmus quietly states.

"Life Wizards"

If you want to find where our life wizards lie,

pay attention to those that have lived long

and still possess candid and innocent hearts.

Their spirits are genuine, playful, and childlike,

their souls are gentle and soaked

in goodness and good faith,

their intent is always noble and transparent

and there is not even an iota of malice

or premeditation in them.

Their personalities

are made out of extraordinary attitudes

Like spontaneity, ingenuity, inspiration,

and most of all, love for life and others.

These kinds of life wizards laugh

plenty and often aloud.

They smile at everyone

and everything whether silly

or profound or simply for no reason at all.

They are also giving and doting, with boundless patience

and tolerance.

They are always ready to serve, help, assist,

educate and rescue.

They are forever at the service of others.

They are humble and wise as well.

This allows them not to take anything

or anyone too seriously,

always looking for the lighter side of people

and things.

Fittingly, these whimsical

and scintillating individuals

are not self-conscious at all about who they are.

Hence, our life's wizards

are always and only defined by others

throughout their lives.

They are also dependable and reliable,

thus, they are the ones who we seek to

lean on, and they provide us with a safe harbor

in the direst of circumstances.

These life sorcerers inhabit a land

where every moment and every person
is precious and irreplaceable.
Their reactions are always measured,
always assuming good faith and giving the benefit
of the doubt first.
And their benevolent
and perennial sunny disposition
usually originates out of their strength of character
and the richness of their virtues and heart.
Additionally, they possess a flawless
and self-regulating "life compass"
that allows them to exercise impeccable judgment
that causes noble reactions regardless of the circumstances
or individuals.
These exceptional fellow life travel companions
always elevate themselves effortlessly
above the mundane.
But above all, their attitude towards life
tells us that no matter how long we have lived,
there are still those that somehow
manage to filter and block out all of the poisons of the spirit,
soul, and heart
that we may encounter along the paths of life.
Life wizards are easy to identify but hard to value
or live with for very long

as they inadvertently may make us feel inadequate.

That is precisely our challenge – how to learn from and

emulate these life sorcerers,

when their intense inner lights

may make ours seem opaque and dark.

So, pay attention to these champions of life

that know how to keep everything in balance

and that find everyone and everything priceless.

Pay attention to these exceptional fellow life companions

– life wizards –

that have the magic formula

of how to live a happy life

while preserving candid and innocent hearts,

for those kinds of old souls

are not frequently found.

"Sometimes dear, you feel like one of those to me," Vicky states as they leave the majestic library.

"I have a long way to go Vicky. There are no shortcuts in life. In order to be a master at anything, one needs to travel the entire road of learning, pay all his dues and burn every candle," states a satisfied young Erasmus.

Royal Cambridge Scholastic Institute (2018)
(University Auditorium)

Professor Cromwell-Smith brings his class back, seemingly from a deep trance.

"Class, life wizards have candid and innocent hearts. They love life and smile at everyone. They have playful souls and don't take anything or anyone too seriously. They're the ones we seek for safe-harbor in the direst of circumstances. For them, every moment and all people are precious and irreplaceable. They always have a sunny disposition and possess the secret of how to be continuously happy," states Professor Cromwell-Smith as he sums it all up.

"We all must learn how to spot these masters of life, as we want to get as close as possible to them, in order to learn and emulate as much as humanly possible from them and learn how to become true wizards in life."

As the professor wraps up his class, a common thought resonates throughout the classroom.

"We already know one professor, we already know one," is the murmur that can be heard as the eminent life wizard heads home.

CHAPTER 8

LIFE AS A JOURNEY

Royal Cambridge Scholastic Institute (2018)
(Erasmus and Victoria's Campus Home)

The raspy voice of Louis Armstrong singing "Smile" awakens her in ecstasy.

'Here we go again,' she realizes while stretching long and lazily. Once more, before her natural inclination for scruffiness kicks in, she finds herself chuckling in joy. Instinctively her eyes pan the room looking for him, and there he is, sitting on one of his two beloved Chesterfields totally absorbed by a book. Then as her eyes adjust to the morning light, she sees them. Lying by his side on an old table are two exquisite orchids – her favorite flower – along with a giant card and a small rectangular box. Her heart is racing and pounding in excitement. She is speechless and just stares at him, seemingly forever.

"I love you dear," she says impulsively. Erasmus lifts his eyes from the book and stares at her with a loving smile and joyful eyes.

"Good morning Victoria, I love you too," he says walking in her direction.

Erasmus leans and kisses her softly on the lips as he places the flowers on the bedside table. He then hands her the card and the tiny small gift box. She opens the card and reads it quickly; "Welcome back to the journey."

"Do you remember when I first asked you something very similar to that?" he teases her.

"Of course dear, at Boston's main train station coming back from our very first trip to Martha's Vineyard. That was the beginning of our journey," she replies in an instant, with a gigantic smile on her face.

She then tears open the wrapping of the gift box and gasps for air in the excitement at the sight. It's a small silver baton encrusted in diamonds on a silver necklace. There is also a small paper strip on the gift box which reads; "Since you already got a ring once, I figured that I may as well give you something that better symbolizes our bond and union." Victoria clings to his neck, her emotions running amok after years of suppression and despair. Erasmus delicately places the necklace on her and whispers in her ear; "Victoria would you marry this infatuated old Brit of yours?"

Victoria trembles and is shaking as tears of joy start pouring out as she places her palms on his face.

"There is nothing else in the world at this moment that I would love to do more than marry you, my dear," she says as he lays her favorite flowers on her lap.

Then, all of a sudden, Victoria turns and pulls out a tiny square box from her bedside table and hands it to him.

"Dear, this little treasure has been waiting for you all along. It's been quite hard for me to keep it from you, but I decided early on that when an occasion like this presented itself, that was going to be the exact right moment to give it to you."

Erasmus is blown away when he first glances at it. It is a charm. "Oh my God!" he calls out as he becomes overcome by emotion. He picks up the mesmerizing charm and once more reads what is carved in it: "Life is a Journey."

"Do you recall who gave us this little treasure?" she asks.

"How couldn't I? The Riddler gave it to us on our second visit," replies Erasmus lost in time while making the decision that such an encounter will be the subject of his class today.

Royal Cambridge Scholastic Institute (2018)
(University Auditorium)

An hour later as Professor Cromwell walks in, he begins with his anecdotal choice of the day.

"Good morning class," states a spirited professor.

"Good morning professor," replies back an equally charged student body.

"Today I'll take you back to the second encounter Vicky and I had with the Riddler. I'm sure you all remember our first visit with Mr. Ringwald where we covered the subjects of life, evolution, and change. The second session with him turned out to be one of the most memorable days of our lives as well."

"It begins like this…"

Boston Marathon (1976)
(Heartbreak Hill)

The young couple has been running for three hours already. It all started smoothly as the first two hours of the run were a gentle downhill. The crowds, the weather, the places, and the sights all contribute to a feeling of euphoria for the two runners. But everything suddenly changes in the third hour. At first, it's almost imperceptible. But soon enough, the gentle but never-ending hill hits them head-on, but they keep on climbing the aptly named "Heartbreak Hill". It's painful and brutal, but running the Boston Marathon in tandem with your loved one is beautiful, inspiring, and makes all the pain and sacrifice worthwhile.

"How are you feeling Vic?" asks Erasmus between breaths.

"Everything aches... my body is screaming at me to stop."

"Hold on a bit longer, we've already done three-quarters of the run."

"When is this hill going to end?"

"It won't Vic, it's going to be like this the rest of the way." A hydration station interrupts their conversation and they both stop briefly to gulp several cups of water. When they finally see the finish line at the end of a long straightaway, on a downtown street, they decide to cross the line holding hands. The clock shows their finishing time just shy of their target of four hours.

After months of preparation, they've done it. But, Erasmus knows that her performance has been, relatively speaking, so much better than his.

"Way to go Vicky, I'm so proud of you; you've just completed 26 miles at a pace just over nine minutes per mile." Vicky chuckles but otherwise doesn't care.

'I'm here just for you my hopelessly incorrigible self-absorbed Brit – to get you out of your shell,' she reflects while literally devouring her second banana whole.

"Erasmus, I've got an idea," she says casually, even though it is something she deliberately planned in advance.

"And what would that be my lady?"

"Why don't we stop by and pay a visit to our new mentor, the Riddler?"

"But, would he be open on a Sunday?"

"What day of the week is today, Erasmus?"

"Sund … oops sorry, I forgot," he states as he really doesn't remember which day of the week it is.

Thanks to the Boston Marathon always being run every year on the third Monday of April, Vicky and Erasmus are able to head towards Mr. Ringwald's open store, in the Boston city center, located just a few blocks from the race's finish line.

Ringwald and Brothers Antiquarians (1976)
(Downtown Boston)

"Mr. Ringwald, how're you this morning?" Erasmus asks as they enter the store.

"How do you think I'm doing? Significant parts of central downtown are totally shut down," the Riddler replies in utter obfuscation. Sensing an agitated state, the running duo quietly sits down and remains in a listening-only mode.

"Were the two of you running in my Monday sales buster?"

"Uh-huh," is the guarded response from the two youngsters.

"How did you do?"

"We arrived at the finish line together, just shy of four hours," replies Erasmus.

"Holding hands," states Victoria, matter of factly.

"What?" the Riddler asks briskly as he is totally insensitive to matters of the heart.

"We arrived at the finish line holding hands," she effusively blurts out again.

The Riddler continues to stare at them with a cranky face. It is a contorted rictus made from lack of sales for the day at his pristine store.

The young couple, tired but candid, slowly disarms him.

"You guys are exhausted and all banged up. Why are you here? Why aren't you home nursing your aches and pains?" the inveterate Riddler asks.

"I'm the guilty one. Since we were in the area to begin with, I asked Erasmus if we could come to see you," Victoria states taking credit.

"And shall I presume that his Royal absentmindedness didn't know today is Monday?" he asks rhetorically.

"How did you know?" she asks in amazement.

"It isn't too hard to figure out. Young Erasmus is rarely here on planet earth," the Riddler says, continuing the roast. As usual, Erasmus simply sports a nutty professor look, utterly oblivious to the Riddler's observations about him.

"The two of you have just been on a 26.2-mile journey where you had to contend with many challenges including the progressive depletion of your body's sources of energy and its capacity to process oxygen efficiently. Today, yours has been a journey that in many ways resembles life."

He starts walking to the far end of the store and at ground level picks up a thin but large book.

"I have here something that I've treasured all my life. Let me read it to you," he says as he walks back, book in hand.

The Riddler starts to read and his words quickly seize them, as they resonate throughout the store.

"Life As A Journey"

We travel through life from the moment

we arrive on planet Earth.

Wherever we are, whatever we do,

we are always going somewhere

as there is always a destination.

155

But, the journey is where life resides,

not the destination.

In so many ways life is like a magnificent, vast,

but perilous ocean.

Our journey is the path we follow,

the wake we leave behind,

accompanied by fellow travelers

that join us along the way.

We are the vessels sailing through it all.

Of all our fellow travelers,

some are better than others.

With many of them, we have a choice

but with others, we don't.

Some are with us for good,

others drop along the way,

but our closest, most loyal,

and beloved companions,

are those that their presence stays with us forever.

Our life's vessel is sturdy and resilient,

but if in addition we trust it, know it,

maintain it, conduct it, will it and love it well,

our ship will be able to withstand

virtually any rogue wave or weather

any storm life throws at us.

Life's journeys occur because we seek to travel,

throughout the entire earth's seas,

in full knowledge that there are endless places

we could discover,

and many more people we may meet.

There are moments in life

when we soar above the oceans and

there are other moments

when we drop all the way to the bottom.

As in life, on an ocean voyage,

we reach countless ports of call,

some picture-perfect, others filled with trappings and

some with rocky shores or dangerous landings.

Sometimes sandy beaches await us,

some others our destination is unbearable

and demands high sacrifices.

On occasion the seas are calm,

the gentle breeze allows for smooth sailing and

on those precious days, the sun is gentle

and the rain is just a drizzle.

Sometimes the oceans display happiness and joy and

on those days the sounds of the seas

feel like a magnificent concerto,

with every instrument playing

the inspiring music of life

with the sky painted in glorious colors and tones.

In these moments,

we seemingly float or walk over water,

we ride the waves, kite the wind, skim the surface,

or dive under it.

On these days we rejoice, celebrate the oceans,

and life's voyage is a joyful ride,

that we wish would never cease to be.

But there are instances when we can barely swim

or even stay afloat as

the seas try to drag us down

with their heaviest ballasts.

On those days the oceans seemingly weep in pain against the

rocks

and the skies drum and lament

in opaque colors of sorrow.

In those moments,

it all seems full of sadness and nostalgia,

yet we resist, vanquish,

and get to live another day.

Sometimes when we are hit by weather systems,

more often than not, after the fact,

we come to the realization that,

preparation, prudence, and alertness,

could or would have prevented it all.

Thus, life's grand travail can be rough and trying.

The ocean's natural elements

may show us their force and strength

as if there was anger and fury bursting out of them.

When this happens, we fight and conquer

by seeking to endure, overcome or outlast them.

When the oceans flip into monsters in an instant,

their waves become voracious destructors

of anything in their sight,

hence, there are no autopilots in life,

neither can we take for granted at any time,

the safe passage of our vessel.

That is why, on a well-traveled life journey,

we appreciate and value the good days

against the bad ones,

as we know the latter will come, sooner or later,

as on the voyage of life, we will experience

birth and love, death and hope, triumph and defeat, faith and
doubt,

wonder and awe, magic and reality, construction, destruction
and reconstruction,

genius and talent, laughter and tears, mediocrity
and tireless efforts,

celebration, and mourning, fame, and repudiation, truth and
falsehood,

health and pain, betrayal and forgiveness,

tragedy and renewal,

passion and humbleness, failure and redemption.

They will come to us on all kinds of days,

weathers and seas.

As the journey moves along,

we will learn again and again that only

love, faith, courage, experience, knowledge, and hope

will see us through the rough patches.

Life's circle is in fact a journey,

we travel endlessly and nonstop,

soaring above or struggling underneath,

through calm or high seas,

through rain or shine,

through countless ports of call.

And we ride, along with travel companions

that join us along the way,

we journey relentlessly,

from beginning to end,

through the oceans of life,

with a restless spirit and a gypsy soul.

"Young Victoria and Erasmus, the sheer power, force, and intensity of the oceans and many of its elements, were elevated in Greek mythology to levels of god and goddesses of the sea. That's how powerful they believed they were. That's why, as with life, we never go against the ocean, to the contrary we harness and absorb its energy to facilitate our journey."

"Vicky here is a lucky charm I've had since my teen years. It bears the name of this writing." The Riddler offers the charm as a parting gift to the bubbly youngsters.

"Life as a Journey," Vicky reads off the charm.

"Thank you, Mr. Ringwald," states both youngsters in unison. Vicky then surprises the Riddler with a kiss of gratitude on both his cheeks as she departs with Erasmus. They both are filled with the joyful inspiration of journeymen leaving their port of call.

Royal Cambridge Scholastic Institute (2018)
(University Auditorium)

Professor Cromwell-Smith brings his class back with a pertinent closing remark.

"We are all embarked on a never-ending perilous and highly rewarding voyage through the course of our lives, and in order to make it through, you all have to trust your vessels. But above all, it's always pertinent to remember that our existential realization and joyful ride resides mainly in life's journey, not on its destination."

"See you all next week."

Then, for an instant, as he leaves, the entire class feels to him like sailors in training and getting their very own ships ready to set sail on their own journey in life. As he glances at them in more detail, he goes away with the feeling that each one of his students feels exactly like him when he was their age, as confident seamen willing and eager to embark on their own existential voyages through the vast ocean of life that lies ahead of them.

CHAPTER 9

OF WEALTH, FAME AND LOVE

Royal Cambridge Scholastic Institute (2018)
(Erasmus and Victoria's Campus Home)

"Dear, ever since you proposed and gave me my precious baton engagement pendant, I've been postponing an important conversation between us," she whispers at him in the early morning hours of the new year. Both are still in bed.

"It couldn't be more transcendental than our previous talk or could it be?" asks Erasmus, once more caught by surprise.

"Well, in some ways it is, but thankfully this one is quite straightforward and less convoluted," says the insecure runaway lover.

"My late husband left a substantial life insurance policy. I plan to set up trust funds for the children with the proceeds. I have a decent amount of savings that includes my retirement account and in a few years, my social security benefits. Meaning – I can support myself," she states in a businesslike manner.

Erasmus listens with benevolent eyes and a mischievous smile.

"Why are you looking at me like that?" she asks feeling uncomfortable with his odd reaction.

"Do you remember the first time you asked me that?" he asks with a bemused expression.

"Of course I do my love, how could I forget?" Victoria replies.

"Vicky, you know how I feel about wealth and material things. And yet, it's wonderful to see you caring for the future of your children in such a way," denotes Erasmus with an unconditionally supportive tone.

"But, I worry that I may not be tending to our own financial security. After all, once I set up the trust we're going to have to depend on what we've got after our careers as educators are over and what I saved from my interrupted stint as a criminal psychologist," she worriedly affirms.

"Victoria, before your wonderful news, I was going to do the same for your kids and I can still do it if you want me to."

Victoria is puzzled and somewhat lost. "Erasmus Cromwell-Smith, do not play games with me on a subject that is so important for my children," states Victoria interrupting him.

"I am dead serious," he declares.

"May I ask how? You're the most unmaterialistic person I've ever met."

"Yes my lady, that's me."

"Well dear, life is quite costly nowadays. But you know what, your intentions are noble, that's what matters and I love you for it," she says, not taking his words seriously, but she couldn't be more wrong.

"Come with me my lady," he says while tenderly taking her hand. Erasmus leads Victoria to their home office and without words, hands her three different folders. She opens the first and her jaw drops in shock.

"I've published some action thrillers and a couple of educational books. Those are just the royalties accumulated over the years," he reveals.

"But I thought you didn't care about ..."

"That's right I still don't like to talk about material wealth, nor do I ever celebrate earning it."

"You've always believed that material riches are not a source of freedom, because you are too aware of its shackles and that's why affluent people never impress you," she remembers.

"Yep, that's right," he agrees while pleasantly surprised about her exacting recollection after so many years.

'Victoria has lived her entire life worrying about having enough to pay the bills, and rightly so, as it's evident that she has never had quite enough. Her challenge now is to do a 180-degree turn and put monetary worries in their right place,' he reasons while staring at her.

"So here I am. Later in life, I have re-encountered my unmaterialistic monk, and he's actually unimaginably wealthy, but he's still the same monk!"

"Vicky, we can do whatever we want to, go places, see the world, meet people, take a long sabbatical. I'll take you everywhere I've been."

"Where is the but in all of this, my love?" she asks.

"That we do all of this while following the same three principles I've lived under all of my life," he declares.

"Wait, I remember them," she says interrupting him.

"Austerity."

"Right on," says Erasmus with a smile.

"Wait, wait, the second one was ..."

"Yes, yes, anonymity," she blurts out.

"Spot on, one to go," he confirms.

"The last one is easy."

"OK spell it then, Vicky."

"Freedom, it is freedom," she declares with pride. "Austerity, anonymity and freedom!"

"Do you remember the first time we ran into those three principles?" he asks.

"What you mean is, the day you adopted them, how couldn't I?" she says teasing him.

"Which was?" he asks.

"It was the same day that we ..." she replies, but suddenly interrupts herself as she remembers. Victoria glances at Erasmus and can immediately feel his desire and excitement.

"So we both have the same recollection?" she asks teasing him as all her passions are also burning.

"Well, there is only one way to find out my dear," he responds delightfully tempting her.

Erasmus approaches her. Then, as he delicately caresses her cheek, his free hand gently pulls her robe open and her unintended moan fills their world with unstoppable lust once again.

A while later when he is ready to leave, Professor Cromwell-Smith realizes he's running late. He's perfectly aware that love in earnest is not compatible at all with the boring rules of time and exacting schedules. And that is how a bit later, for the first time in his life, he suffers the ignominious embarrassment of being five minutes late to the beginning of his sacrosanct lecturing ritual. Today, he does not care one bit. He's in love and all he feels is effusiveness and impulsiveness in his state of utter bliss.

Royal Cambridge Scholastic Institute (2018)
(University Auditorium)

"Hi," he sheepishly greets his audience.

"Ahem," the collective clearing of the throats response is heard from the student body calling him out on his tardiness.

"We understand professor," states a group of students standing up as if making excuses for him.

"Please accept my apologies; I am not setting the right example today. But, even though, undeservedly so, I will still demand punctuality from you all," states a heartfelt professor.

"We told you professor that we understand," another small group calls out teasing him.

Now he is puzzled and a bit embarrassed. So, when the next interruption occurs, it rattles him.

"A little bird told us," states another small group of students.

"What?" the professor asks, now totally at a loss.

"A little bird arrived earlier than you and told us you were going to be late. She said you were going to take us to a place today that she wanted to relive and would not miss it for the world," states a well-rehearsed foursome.

Professor Cromwell-Smith pans the room and spots her right away. She is standing in the middle of the crowd.

"I am right here. Right here my love," she states with her persona in déjà vu.

Totally infatuated by her presence, the professor struggles mightily to pull himself together, remain circumspect in one piece, and show the proper decorum his audience deserves. Finally, breathing deep followed by an almost imperceptible sigh, he smiles and winks at his soul mate.

"Class, today I'm going to take you back in time some forty-plus years ago, to a day, when Vicky and I received a very particular invitation, that sent us into an exhilarating ride of discovery and wisdom that has lasted a lifetime."

"It starts like this…"

Harvard (1976)
(Victoria and Erasmus's Studio)

"Erasmus are we going to accept the invitation or not?" asks a slightly exasperated Vicky.

"I don't know. What do you think?" he replies evasively.

"Don't ask the same question every time, and don't try to be a Riddler as there is only one in the New England antiquarian world, and it isn't you," she snaps back in utter exasperation.

"Well, I'm thinking about it," he says giving excuses.

"How much longer dear? That's pretty much the same response I get from you every time I ask," she says sarcastically.

"I'll make my mind up soon," he volunteers unconvincingly.

"You better or we'll miss it," she warns.

Erasmus opens the card once more and reads it. "Invitation: You are cordially invited to meet with a select group of antiquarians from all over the country. A limited number of ancient books will be exhibited as well. Dinner and cocktails will be served."

'Why is he vacillating? What's all the fuss about? He should be dying to go. Normally, he would accept an invitation like this, in the blink of an eye, as this is a subject he obsesses about, but he is not doing so now – why?' wonders Victoria struggling to find an answer and a solution.

Impulsively, she walks over to him, yanks the card away, and starts to read it once more. In fact, she reads it aloud twice but draws a blank from Erasmus. 'Why?' she wonders while reading the bottom of the card where formalities like address, attire, hour and date appear. She would love to wear her Sunday dress around such erudite. Then, all of a sudden it hits her, while her eyes are fixated on the address. She puts the card down and faces him.

"It's the address, isn't it? All this fuss, just because it's a rich man's address?"

He doesn't respond.

"Well, I'm accepting the invitation and I don't care whether you come or not," she states not really meaning it.

Antique Book's Exhibit Reception,
Boston Suburbs (1976)

"Erasmus we've been here for barely an hour and you've already managed to alienate all three of the event hosts, who I should add, are among the richest men not only in New England but in the entire country. What's wrong with you?" asks an irritated Victoria.

"Material wealth does not impress me. I have no respect for a false sense of superiority or banal arrogance from ignorant, deeply miserable, and unhappy people," declares a pompous Erasmus.

"But they made this possible. They paid for it," states a cautious Vicky.

"And for that, I'm extremely grateful and have heartfeltly expressed it to each one of them," Erasmus acknowledges.

"Where did you get all of this British working-class resentment?" asks a puzzled Victoria.

"Actually, we do quite well on our lovely island with real people, a rich life, and boundless literary wealth, thank you," he replies defensively.

"Then your highness, no wealthy man in the world would deserve your appreciation and respect?" states a sarcastic Victoria.

"Oh yes, some of them do, but as I said they are a rare breed to find Vic," says Erasmus matter of factly.

"OK, give me an example," snaps back Victoria.

"I'll give you one – Andrew Carnegie – a Scottish-American entrepreneur and philanthropist. In order to understand his greatness, one must study him. Specifically, look at the following five dimensions: How many of the institutions he created for the betterment of humanity are still in existence today nearly six decades after his death; How many people in this country still benefit today from his deeds?; At what age did he start to give back to society?; What percentage of his wealth did he give back while alive?; What percentage of it did he give back when he died?" lectures Erasmus.

"But wasn't he a ruthless businessman?" asks Victoria

"You see Vic, it's not about the mercantile prowess and hoarding abilities of these very wealthy individuals. It's about the quality and quantity of their lasting contributions to society," Erasmus elaborates further.

"Excuse me, may I interrupt?" states a rather excessively skinny and tall man with a sunken face and a hanging suit much bigger than his frame.

"We're having a private conversation if you don't mind," states Erasmus annoyed but with a hint of curiosity at the Scottish accent.

"Well, it's very poor etiquette and unacceptable bad manners for me to interrupt such a lively conversation, but it's even more inexcusable that in addition, albeit unintentionally, that I've overheard most of it, especially when you mentioned the name of a fellow countryman, the Lilliputian giant from Dunfermline, the greatest Scotsman that ever lived."

Erasmus and Vicky are transfixed not really knowing how to react.

"Who are you sir?" asks Erasmus.

"Colin Carnegie."

"Are you...? presses Erasmus.

"Yes, I am Andrew's distant relative," replies Mr. Carnegie.

"No, I mean are you the famous antiquarian from Edinburgh?"

"Yes, at your service. I have locations in Glasgow and Inverness as well thank you."

"And you young man? You are from Wales, let me guess, Cardiff?"

"Wales yes, but Hay-on-Wye," Erasmus replies to a wide-eyed and delighted, nodding and smiling, Scottish antiquarian.

Victoria realizes that Erasmus is on the verge of obsessing into his favorite field.

"Youngsters, you've struck gold today, as I'm going to share with you a scribble that pertains in an exacting fashion to your points of discussion. I am certain it'll enrich and shed even more light on your discussion."

"Would you like me to read it to you?" asks Mr. C.

"Yes, please," replies an enthusiastic Erasmus while Vicky looks on dejected as she feels that an opportunity has been lost tonight. She will soon find out that she couldn't be more wrong. The lanky man pulls a scroll from his balloonist coat and quickly seizes their attention and takes them into another world.

"Of Wealth, Fame and Love"

In one way or another,

we all chase,

some of us relentlessly,

wealth, fame and love,

in this exact order of importance.

But these life illusions

don't always present themselves

in such a prescribed pecking order.

Fact is, we never know

who shows up first,

or if any of them

will ever make itself present at all.

But if they do,

we'll face one of life's most puzzling conundrums,

that is, what we are keenly after,

is not only elusive,

but usually comes

at the expense of something else.

Correspondingly, more often than not,

when we are graced with riches and a good name,

it comes at the expense of love,

or if we become wealthy,

it is at the expense of the other two,

or a good reputation comes without love or riches,

or love blesses us without riches

or even a good name.

What is not so apparent though,

is that this mirage triad of grand illusions,

we covet so much, comes at the expense of others,

even more important virtues,

some existential in nature, other, crucial life attitudes,

than our three grand illusory obsessions.

As we go after wealth,

we sacrifice frugality,

and run the risk of losing

our ability to appreciate

the true value of people or material things,

or perhaps even worse

we may become unable

to value the simplest of things,

especially those that

are nominally scarce in quantifiable magnitudes.

As we go after reputation,

we run the risk that,

nothing about us is nameless any longer,

and the fiction of what others think about us,

morphs into an obsession

and becomes more important

than the reality of who we really are.

Falsely, anonymity then becomes

a synonym with failure or lack of accomplishment,

and everything we do or we work for,

becomes attached to our name and ego.

But the biggest risk we run with fame

is that everything we do in life,

for others or ourselves,

becomes somewhat and somehow,

driven and conditioned,

by what others think, how they react,

and how they behave.

Thus, we lose part or all of our sense of identity,

as the purest of all acts in life,

the acts of conscience,

where we are only accountable to ourselves,

totally escape us.

But the most difficult

of our life grand illusions to go after is love

as by doing so,

we run the risk of sacrificing freedom.

Love is a compromise between two souls,

where each one "gives in" a part of themselves,

and a couple is born.

But a twosome is a separate unit

from the two individuals,

and the balance between

the individuality of each one and the couple,

even though attainable,

is very difficult to achieve,

and even more so to maintain.

The problem lies in,

that self-determination and liberty

are not that compatible with love.

It takes a lot of maturity and tolerance

for both to coexist.

It is perhaps in true love

where the boundaries within a couple blend best.

This happens,

when freedom, instead of being an obstacle,

is actually the bond,

that unites authentic love,

then strings and ties,

are not driven by walls

of insecurity and possession,

but by the natural,

spontaneous and comfortable longing,

for our other half,

and the certainties of immanent belonging

to someone else's heart.

Are we then, just chasing,

these three grand illusions in life?

Is that all we are able to do?

But, are they only a mirage?

Do we sacrifice frugality and austerity

when we go after riches and wealth?

Do we lose anonymity and our own identity

when we are after reputation and a good name?

And, do we lose freedom and self-determination

when we go after love?
Perhaps we should learn to be frugal and austere first
so we learn the true value of things,
and the preciousness of each fellow human being,
before chasing wealth.
And we should learn how to be
humbly anonymous and modestly nameless first,
and do things for ourselves,
based on our conscience alone,
before chasing reputation and a good name,
which are always based
on what other's think of us,
instead of on what we really think about ourselves.
And we could learn about freedom
and self-determination first,
hopefully before true love finds us,
and we hook up with someone else,
so we would be able to balance,
the emerging couple
with our individuality and sense of being.
Life is a mirage of three grand illusions,
wealth, fame and love,
that require a fine balance between them,
as not to hurt some,
at the expense of a triad of others,

namely frugality, anonymity, and freedom

as we require them as well,

for a wholesome, well-balanced, and happy life.

As the Scotsman finishes reading, he contemplates the young couple who are wearing benign eyes filled with deep satisfaction.

Mr. Carnegie, we will be in debt to you for the rest of our lives," states a new Vicky, feeling closure through newly acquired wisdom.

"Austerity, anonymity, and freedom will be my guiding principles from now on," states Erasmus promising to keep in touch forever with the man from the Scottish highlands.

As they get ready to go, the young couple is finally relaxed and playful.

(Victoria and Erasmus' Studio)

"Why are you looking at me like that?" she quizzically asks as they enter their small studio.

"Vic there is nothing more sensual for me than a beautiful woman in Katherine Hepburn flats moving with self-confidence, grace and exuding absolute ease and comfort with herself in every gesture, glance, and posture. I find it the epitome of femininity," he replies.

"Why?" she asks.

"I love it when a lady does not really care about her height, when seemingly, such banality, is totally irrelevant to her, he answers with pleasure.

"But am I short?" she presses in doubt and wounded vanity.

"Inevitable reaction, right? My fault, sorry, no. Vicky, you aren't and you know it. But don't you see it, height is precisely not the point," he reassures her, but she's hardly listening as the sensual feeling of the flats she is wearing has her totally snared in his poetic nets.

"So my lady, what was your original question, again?" he asks with a subtle subliminal message of affirmation.

And as she answers, he leads them both, holding hands, into their never-ending world of passion, sparked and driven by healthy tensions and differences of opinions and always spiked by Victoria's vivacious and spontaneous personality, perennially radiant in her Katherine Hepburn flats.

Royal Cambridge Scholastic Institute (2018)
(University Auditorium)

"Professor Cromwell-Smith brings back his class to the present and with a broad smile on his face stares directly into his true love's eyes.

Delighted to have joined him on this day, Vicky is in a trance while nodding and holding her hands on her heart.

"Class, take this with you forever. What is austerity to wealth? What is anonymity to fame? And what is freedom to love?"

"I want you all to know that your professor is still the same person today as he was when I went away. He truly lives within the principles that were analyzed in that poem," Vicky says with conviction and totally oblivious to the fact that her joyous and opportune enthusiasm has literally interrupted, albeit to no consequence, the end of his class.

This time, it's his turn to thank her with both hands wrapped around his heart, as well.

"See you all next week," he says in satisfaction.

Several discussion groups remain in the auditorium as Erasmus and Victoria leave holding hands. From afar many notice that they seem duly inoculated against life's three grand illusions.

CHAPTER 10

OF FAMILY, TRUE FRIENDSHIP
AND LOVE

Royal Cambridge Scholastic Institute (2019)
(Erasmus and Victoria's Campus Home)

Still living at their old home, Victoria's three young adult children, Elizabeth-Victoria 24, the oldest, Bartholomew 22, the one in the middle, and Sarah 19, the youngest, show up to visit with their mom before heading for a long weekend on Nantucket Island with a group of friends. They surprise their mother, walking in unannounced as she is having breakfast, but she already knows about it as her kids are simply responding to hints she has dropped here and there about this particular morning. Nevertheless, Victoria is ecstatic to see her kids all together. She finally has the three of them in one place as she wants to share the news she has been keeping to herself.

"Erasmus asked me to marry him," she announces hesitantly.

"Congratulations mom!" is the collective response from her kids. Victoria shows them the distinctive and beautiful engagement baton. "When did he propose?" asks Sarah as both sisters inspect the precious jewel. Bart, on the other hand, is trying to figure out what the strangely looking item means.

"Not long ago, he surprised me with it," Victoria declares, beaming.

"Why a baton?" asks Bart.

"It's something very symbolic in both our lives," she explains.

"Oh, the tale of the broken baton!" blurts Bart, finally getting it – the story they all have heard countless times since they were kids.

"Why did you wait to tell us mom?" asks Sarah.

Silence ensues as Victoria struggles to find the right words.

"I guess that, I wanted to make sure it was real," Victoria says, a bit contrite.

"What did you answer?" asks Elizabeth.

"I said yes, with all of my heart," Victoria states spontaneously while realizing it's a bitter-sweet moment for her kids.

"Mom, can you finally stop feeling guilty, once and for all. How many times do we have to tell you that this is something we all want for you," states Bart in very clear terms.

Her three kids gather around and hug her in joy. They all cry a little, then start to smile in what still remains a hard to figure and process moment for the family.

"Now, we all look forward to a new life and a new family," states a spirited Elizabeth.

"What are your long-range plans, then?" asks Bart.

"We're all going to live in this house. I have put our, soon-to-be, former home on the market and plan to move each of you over here. If you're asking yourselves why not the other way around, the reason is simple, our teaching jobs are close by and it cuts out the one-hour commute," states Victoria matter of factly. And, to her great relief, all she sees are faces of consent from all of them.

"Additionally, there's something equally transcendental that you need to know. I'm going to set up trust funds, one for each one of you, with the proceeds of the life insurance policy your father left," she announces to her children's obvious surprise.

"Mom, but what about you?" asks a suddenly worried Sarah.

"I have my savings, retirement plan and in the not so distant future, my social security. Modest but enough."

"What about the professor?" asks Bart.

"Well at first, I assumed that he, as a pedagogue, would have a similar situation as mine. But he completely surprised me. Let me give you a little bit of background. As you all know, he is a bachelor who never married or had any kids. So, he told me that he was thinking of setting up trust funds for you guys. Well, it turns out that my beloved professor, the most unmaterialistic person I've ever known, is wealthy beyond imagination, thanks to royalties from several action-thrillers and educational books he has published over the years."

"I hope his money doesn't interfere with your relationship," interjects Bart.

"No, it won't I'm sure. A modern woman must live off what she and her spouse earn together, even if her only job is at home. It is all about self-respect, always remember that kids," Victoria states.

"Ok mom, he's obviously not around – where are you hiding him? Where is he? We all want to talk to him," states Bart.
"I'm sorry to disappoint you, he's on his way to class. He'll be back before noon though."

Royal Cambridge Scholastic Institute (2019)
(Faculty Building)

As he parks his old rusty bike, Professor Cromwell-Smith is worried sick. Last night, Victoria told him that her three children would be visiting her this morning. 'Why just her and not us?' he thought. 'Are they supportive of our relationship? Neither of them has yet flown out of the family's nest. Do they approve of their mom not living at their family home any longer? Would they move in as per their mom's wishes?' he goes on to muse, arguing back and forth inside his own head.
'They were aware of their mother's feelings and knew almost everything about our time together as youngsters at Harvard, as well as my life before I met their mom, thanks to the stories she related to them, over and over,' he continues to ponder.
As he walks through the hallways of the main faculty building, he remains in a state of turmoil and fear, until suddenly, it dawns on him. 'You silly old man, she is informing them about your

proposal,' he reflects as his face brightens. As he walks the corridors of the educational institution duty takes over. 'Family.' That'll be today's subject.

"Good morning everyone," he announces, greeting the student body with gusto.

"Good morning professor," they respond in unison.

"Today, we'll revisit a moment back in time where family made itself present in our lives."

"It begins like this ..."

"Harvard (1977)"

"Erasmus, my folks are very traditional people from mid-western America."

"That's OK, I'm looking forward to getting to know them."

"I'm not sure the feeling is going to be mutual," she abruptly interjects.

Erasmus is shocked by Victoria's remark.

"Why would you say that?" he asks with a puzzled look.

"I don't think it's anything particularly negative about you or that it's even personal, after all, they don't know you at all," she states rebutting him.

"Exactly, he responds," but his words only draw a blank stare from Vicky.

"So, what is it then?" he asks partly talking to himself.

"I guess they only see me marrying someone from my hometown and more specifically someone from the same congregation. Anything else is something they simply cannot fathom," she argues.

"Why would they let you come to Harvard then?" he asks.

"They almost didn't. But I earned it academically, so in the end, they had to let me come," she replies.

"There you have it, perhaps they are more open-minded than you think," he argues in a pointless effort.

"I'm afraid not, they expect me to come back," predictably she answers.

"But you're an adult Victoria. Anyhow, what matters is what you want. What is it?" A frustrated Erasmus now asks.

"I want nothing else but to be with you," she says as they kiss in earnest.

"Wonderful, when do I get to meet them?" he asks naively.

"Sometime in the future, but not now," she answers. Letting the shoe drop.

"What? Why?" Erasmus is totally lost!

"They don't know we are living together dear and knowing you, I see no way to avoid you blurting it out while exhibiting your lovely British sense of being proper and exacting on all of your statements, and in particular, on all your responses. And Erasmus, don't even suggest it, because I won't ask you to lie," she reasons with finality.

"Then don't introduce me as your boyfriend but as a classmate or whatever you want," he pleads once more. However, he senses a brick wall.

"Not now, but perhaps at some point," she replies in a cursory fashion.

"I think you are drowning in thought and making this bigger than what it is Victoria," he laments to no avail.

Sure enough, shortly after Vicky welcomes her parents into town and instead of getting to know the place, they spend long hours arguing with their daughter about completing her studies closer to home. Sadly, a couple of days later, her parents leave without an introduction, so, utterly troubled by the events but especially her behavior, he decides to take Victoria with him and seek wisdom on the subject of family with one of their trusted mentors, Thomas Albert Faith, who in Erasmus' opinion, is best suited for their query.

Riverside Village, Boston Suburbs (1977)
(Mr. Faith's Antique Book Store)

"Victoria and Erasmus, Mr. F at your service. How can I be of help?" says a spirited Mr. Faith.

"Mr. F we're seeking enrichment including how to interact and deal with family."

"What is the nature of the problem you're trying to solve?"

"Victoria," responds Erasmus passing the buck.

At first, she hesitates but eventually gathers the strength to begin, but all the way through the story, Victoria is embarrassed as she tries to narrate the problem with her parents.

Mr. Faith quickly springs into a fast walk towards the back of the store and they follow. Mr. F enters what appears to be his office and as they come in as well, they see it – a small elevator behind a wooden sliding door. Together they go down one floor and upon arrival they literally face a bank vault door, which takes just a few seconds for Mr. F to open.

"This building used to be a bank, before I bought it two decades ago."

As the inside of the vault comes into view, Erasmus gets bug eyes as he glances around. There are hundreds of mammoth books and their condition and covers quickly indicate to him that they're in the presence of a timeless and priceless collection. At the center of the absolutely dry and perfectly tempered room, there's a small conference table. Fluorescent lights provide intensely white illumination.

"Have a seat." Mr. Faith invites.

He then proceeds to select an enormous, ancient book. He places it right on top of the table and opens it. There's a ribbon marker already in place, right where he wants it to be.

"The two of you are pointing in the wrong direction. You are reacting against interventionism and interference, which is a natural reaction to your parents' fear of losing you, Victoria."

"We're consenting adults, they have no right to choose what life Vicky is going to live, much less who she is allowed to love or form a family with," Erasmus protests.

Her eyes widen in surprise as this is the first time he has mentioned the word family between them. She likes it and fears it at the same time.

"Perhaps you should broaden your view of the situation?" states Mr. F.

"How?" asks Erasmus.

"It's not only about family," replies Mr. F a bit cryptically.

"What do you mean?" presses Erasmus.

"First of all, those we hold dear, encompass a large group which includes not only family but true friends and all matters of the heart as well. Once you understand who is who, in your closest circles in life, the fundamental questions become, what are we supposed to do? What is expected of us? What are the boundaries we have to set and vice versa?" Mr. F reasons in wisdom.

Erasmus gazes back at the eccentric antiquarian with gratitude and curiosity.

"I must caution you though. This writing does not read like a poem or an essay. It's more like a manifesto."

The young couple is completely taken by Mr. Faith's words as they listen to his every remark with undivided attention.

"It was written as a declaration with a series of ideals where enunciated," states Mr. F.

"You mean like the Declaration of Independence?" asks Victoria in splendorous naiveté.

"Certainly, in that vein, but limited to the matters of love, true friendship, and family. So, be aware that this ancient scribble is an enunciation of the duties, responsibilities, rights, and boundaries in regard to those matters. It's a set of aspirations and ideals to follow in regard to our relationships with those closest to us," the erudite mentor concludes, completing the introduction. Mr. Faith then starts to read in earnest.

"Of Family, True Friendship and Love"

In all matters of family, true friendship and love,

reside all of those that are dearest and nearest to us,

as well as,

the bonds that hold them together.

The tight closeness and indivisible unity

of these three existential bonds

are one of the most important sources of strength

and happiness in our lives.

But we can never be careful enough,

as once the closeness and tightness

of these bonds is lost,

it is extremely trying and difficult to recover them.

That is why, we always defend and protect

our walls of intimacy,

as closeness and tightness are not immanent,

but have to be earned

through daily work and sacrifices

that we put into family, true friendship, and love.

The power and strength of these bonds,

originate out of sticking together as a whole irrespective of

anything or anyone.

Happiness and joy ensue, from the intimacy and closeness of

living in full,

along with those we love or who are dear to us.

All of our actions, on matters of family,

true friendship, and love

are driven by acts of conscience,

where we are accountable to ourselves first,

and act because our conscience dictates so,

not because we are conditioned or limited

by what those closest to us do, say or think.

But the boundaries between what we must do

and what is expected of us and vice versa,

in matters of the heart, true friendship, and family,

are at best tenuous, and more than likely moving targets or

even shifting sands.

This, unless we are willing and able to formulate

and enunciate a declaration,

in a way a manifesto that dresses us,

with the sacred mantle

of these preciously existential bonds,

while at the same time,

casting in stone with sufficient clarity,

what is it exactly, that we pursue?

It reads as follows:

Together,

We love unlimitedly with all there is in our hearts,

We are fiercely and infinitely loyal,

We always pursue and preserve unity,

We conduct ourselves with impeccable dignity,

We defend and maintain the integrity of our honor,

We incessantly and humbly pray

in the practice of our faith,

We treasure each and every precious memory

and moment,

We never surrender the power of hope,

We never, ever leave unfinished business,

neither quit, jump ship,

abandon, run away, waver, flicker,

break ranks, or voluntarily leave anyone behind,

And if we fail, we fall together,

but always get back up.

Again and again, again and again.

Then,

As life's paths and careers brew and unfold

into tangible efforts of personal growth,

deliberate undertakings, or simply projects underway,

We nurture, prepare, support, exalt, motivate,

believe in, assist, lift, cheer, set, guide, tender,

advise, steer, stick with, inspire,

role model, praise, teach with endless patience,

and are always there, available at any time,

when we are needed.

When in other circumstances,

we are required to intervene

and get involved swiftly and decisively,

We confront, level with, admonish, claim to,

protest to, complain to,

refute, dissent from, contradict, oppose,

prevent, save, avoid,

change directions from, rectify, listen well,

and even if within grasp, forbid outright.

On other occasions when we are tested inside out

and our virtues and values,

especially our integrity and capacity to give

are challenged to extremes.

In those moments,

we hoist high up the shiny flag of the truth
and above all,
have boundless patience, are always ready to respond,
have sound tolerance for, offer generous wisdom to,
behave with compassion for,
act with composure and moderation for,
are ready to give and share what we have,
dependably fulfill all our promises and commitments
and always respect and value others.
When we err or make mistakes,
we are contrite, make amends,
repent, seek atonement for,
and are always ready to forgive and be forgiven.
Etiquette, decorum, and true respect
are not only expected
but also required from all of us, therefore,
We never yell, curse, shout, scream,
humiliate, insult, derogate,
hurt, sink, put down, seek revenge,
judge, or criticize others.
We shall seek to be a role model
by being perennially humble,
thus,
We pursue frugality, modesty,
discretion, and moderation.

Breeding the new generations is part of our duties,

thus,

We always, provide, train, teach, hold accountable,

Inculcate, assign responsibility

and invest in one another.

But above all, we never lose perspective

about the simple things in life,

therefore,

Sweet or painful, we always tell the truth.

We laugh and enjoy,

We smile and have fun, rejoice and share happiness.

And together we acclaim and celebrate

a life of Love, True Friendship and Family.

"Victoria and Erasmus, on matters of love, true friendship, and family we are like Dumas' three musketeers, all for one and one for all. And the catalogue of everything we are supposed to do and want to be is dense and comprehensive but in no instance reflects or grants the right for us to govern those three constituencies. Victoria you are a free consenting adult. Thus, only you can decide about your life," concludes the erudite mentor.

"Thank you, Mr. F, we will be in debt to you for the rest of our lives," Erasmus tells him in gratitude as the rattled couple heads for the train station. Erasmus rides the train back to Harvard full of confidence and relieved as a big cloud may have been removed from their life. Victoria, on the other hand, is full of doubts and feels pushed into a corner.

'My parents only want what is best for me,' she reasons, oddly trying to defend them against her enamored self.

Royal Cambridge Scholastic Institute (2019)
(University's Auditorium)

Professor Cromwell-Smith comes back to the present with a worried face as his old insecurities from the past are back. Rationally, he knows better as they are all unfounded. But his fears overwhelm him. Suddenly, he has a strong urge to see her and to the surprise of his entire class, the venerable professor leaves, rather abruptly barely waving and whispering to himself.

"See you all next week."

Then, as he exits the auditorium, he almost runs head-on into her.

"Vicky," he smiles in relief.

"You're certainly in a hurry today dear," she says smiling. But in a fraction of a second, she sees the intense fear in his eyes. From then onwards, her instincts take over. She tenderly covers his face with both palms of her hands, and then looking at him up close, she reassures him once more.

"I'm here you old fool. I'm not going anywhere," she lovingly states, with teary but determined eyes.

"Please don't stop doing so, my lady," he pleads as he relaxes a bit.

"As long as it takes, as many times as it is required, I will continue to do so my dear," she reassures him once more.

"Now, into other matters, I need to talk to you about my kids," she announces. Erasmus' eyes start to widen again so she abruptly states, "no panic needed my love, it's wonderful news." As the loving couple heads away, the auditorium remains packed with students, still immersed on the profoundness of the subject covered by their eminent professor. Many of the students start evaluating, others reassessing their family, friends, and their bonds, ties, and boundaries while contrasting them to what they've just learned.

CHAPTER 11

LIFE AS A CIRCUS

Royal Cambridge Scholastic Institute (2019)
(Erasmus and Victoria's Campus's Backroads)

The night before, Victoria and Erasmus had a spirited evening which included a splendid dinner at a family-owned New England seafood restaurant. It was a memorable event as the infatuated couple finally experienced her kids' acceptance. In the end, what really mattered to her children the most, was to see their mom with a spark in her eyes, totally relaxed around Erasmus, and above all, truly, truly happy.

"Dear you were wonderful last night," she declares in joy, as they pedal through the campus's back roads.

"And I should add, they love you very, very much my lady," he affirms spiritedly, as he zigzags playfully with his old rusty bike through the colors of the early spring.

Victoria looks at him feeling proud and unburdened.

"You wouldn't remember, by any chance, when I first became enamored with the idea of being a mom and having children?" she asks while teasing him with subtle certainty of his ignorance.

"Well, the only time I can recall you mentioning something about it, was at the circus," he answers promptly.

Victoria breathes hard, with surprised eyes, and an empathetic heart that values his sensitive memory of such a transcendental moment in her life.

"It was actually quite fortunate that on that particular day we went to the circus," she says teasing him.

"Quite deliberate, I would say. You'd planned it all along," an amused Erasmus replies, not falling for it.

Professor Cromwell is so lost in his own thoughts that only the jostling of his bike hitting a bump on the road, just short of his faculty building, brings him back to reality.

"The circus, that'll be today's subject," he voices with sudden inspiration.

Then, after hurriedly mounting Victoria's bike on their car's rack and sending her off to her own classes at Boston University, with a soft, warm kiss, the professor walks into class, with his head filled with the world of traveling artists performing for the patrons inside of a tent.

Royal Cambridge Scholastic Institute (2019)
(University's Auditorium)

"Good morning class."

"Good morning professor."

"Last week, I was distraught by a domestic affair, so I left rather abruptly, please accept my apologies," he explains apologetically.

"Is everything okay at home, professor?" asks an incredulous bunch in unison.

The professor is startled and looks at them with an uncomfortable expression.

"What are you all up to?"

Then it dawns on him just before he is roasted.

"Many of us saw the Shakespearean scene, at the doorstep of the auditorium last week professor," the same group states.

A bit embarrassed he cuts them off.

"Enough roasting of your professor this morning," he says without much conviction in his voice.

He then sees the expectant looks in the crowd and bends to their will.

"All right you guys, nothing happened, as a surprise, Victoria wanted to greet me at the door right when I left class – she did and it was wonderful," explains the professor while flashing a huge reassuring smile.

'They all care about my well-being,' he reasons as he gazes at the crowd with eyes of gratitude. Protocol quickly takes over and the professor is all business in an instant.

"Today, I am going to take you back to the day that Victoria and I found and acquired lots of wisdom after we visited a circus. It begins like this ..."

"New York City (1977)"

Harvard has just played Princeton and as usual, Vicky lit the field up with her baton maneuvers and magic. As they exit the stadium, Victoria turns towards Erasmus and says, "please take me to the store in New York City where you bought me the baton."

A little while later on during the short train ride from New Jersey to NYC, Erasmus scratches his head in thoughts. 'Why would she want me to take her over there?'

Soon they find themselves walking while holding hands, through the streets of Manhattan and the beauty of the autumn colors in Central Park.

'Somehow this is very important to her,' he reasons.

Entering the park through 69th Street and 5th Avenue, they stroll across the grass and walk with a carefree attitude. The two youngsters' love exuberance is matched by the tightness of their hand-holding and the incessant free-spirited goofiness of their actions. They chase pigeons at the pond, plaster their faces in ice cream at the fountain, spill popcorn on each other at strawberry fields, and release dozens of balloons into the sky just before Poet's Row.

"Maybe one day you'll be an iconic poet honored with a statue like these," Vicky suddenly blurts out with candid eyes and a hopeful smile while contemplating the figures honoring great poets.

The sight of her, innocent, beautiful, and dreaming big way into the future, inspires him.

"Why not?" he replies with the same ingenuity.

That's when the magic happens and he starts to do an improvised recitation without taking his eyes off of her.

"Let's call it …"

"One Verse at Poets' Row"

"As the leaves drop
at Poets' Row,
I see your eyes sparkle
in the hues of the fall.
The gentle breeze whistles
as the spirit of "The Big Apple"
spreads to every corner
of the city's lungs.
The park is colored
with endless tones
of yellows and oranges
and why not?
Bits of reds as well,
seemingly all, just for you,
my love.
But it is in this hallow corner
where your smile shines the most,
as your head full of dreams
realizes,
that your heart has been taken,
on an autumn's romance,

by the spirit of the park

and by my very own,

while I recite this verse

made out of precious fallen leaves

and my infatuated heart and soul."

Vicky extends her arms and deliberately pulls him close and tight to her, and while she kisses him effusively all over, her words are soft but firm, coming from a determined and enamored soul.

"My heart is completely and utterly taken my love," she says surrendering to his verse at Poet's Row. Then they talk non-stop as if they had not seen each other for years. When they finally exit the southwest corner of the park on Columbus Circle, they're soaked in Central Park bliss and the Big Apple's magical spirit.

After one more carefree and longer walk through the city streets, Erasmus is shocked when they enter the store and Vicky spends no more than five minutes inside.

"For me, this place symbolizes your declaration of love. It was the over-the-cliff moment where your grand gesture won my heart over. Once I learned that you had traveled overnight to get me a replacement for my broken baton, I became possessed with a willingness to move mountains, go anywhere or do anything for you Erasmus. Even though at the time, I didn't know who did it, I prayed and prayed with all my heart for that angel to be you," she says in high spirits. Victoria leans and kisses Erasmus effusively. She stands on one leg while the other is bent upwards as a parting marine's woman kiss.

"There's another reason I brought you over here dear. Take a look at the address of the musical instrument shop." She hands him a business card: The World of Marching Bands Instruments – the largest store of its kind on planet earth, NY, NY (behind the Madison Square Garden). Then, she shows him a newspaper clipping: Ringling Brothers performing at the Madison Square Garden in New York during the months of September through December 1977.

"I want you to take me to the circus," she pleads with the expression of a little girl. Erasmus obliges with ease as they simply cross the street and proceed to have the time of their lives. A couple of hours later as they leave the arena, Erasmus is the one who takes the initiative.

"Let's take the train and go pay a visit to Mr. L in New Haven."

"All right, but under one condition," she replies.

"You want to eat at the French Bistro," he replies back, reading her mind.

"Bistro and Boulangerie, dear," she says as she's already tasting the French pastries in her mind.

On the ride over Vicky makes a memorable remark. "Dear, today at the circus, viewing so many children's happy faces, for the first time in my life, I felt this overwhelming desire to have children and someday become a mother," she says with heartfelt desire.

Erasmus holds Victoria tight to his chest and dreams alongside. But, out of shyness and ignorance, he says nothing. This does not go unnoticed to Vicky and fatefully she totally misreads his good heart.

New Haven, CT (1977)

Their host, Mr. Lafayette, lights up when he sees them enter the store. 'He may be three generations away from France but he's still 100 percent French to me,' thinks Victoria observing his body language, mannerisms, and clothing.

"To what do I owe the immense pleasure of your august presence at my humble Athenaeum today?" quizzes the pompous tall antiquarian.

The young couple hesitates with a response to his bombastic question.

"There isn't a game in town this weekend, right?" being himself he asks, switching from a flowery greeting into a mundane question.

"Harvard played at Princeton so we took the train from New Jersey," Victoria replies.

"A fair ride just to visit your argumentative antiquarian," Mr. L declares.

"We both wanted to see you. We were at Madison Square Garden for the circus earlier in the day," states Victoria.

"And?" Mr. L quizzes in anticipation of the real reason for their visit.

"We were wondering if you would have any ancient scribble relative to the circus in general or perhaps about one in particular?" queries Erasmus.

Mr. L contemplates the question for what seems an eternity. Slowly, a smile of certainty takes a hold of him.

"Yes I do and it's one of my favorite readings. I'll be right back," he replies as he walks away with impossibly long strides. Accordingly, he takes forever and a long time later shows up full of dust and dirt.

"Sorry, but this one was hard to find. It was worth it because I have here with me the perfect reading for your wishes," the antiquarian states without a clue as to how long he took on his quest. Mr. Lafayette then starts to read in earnest ...

"Life as a Circus"

Life is like a circus

with the same exact cast of characters

popping out of its book pages.

We are surrounded by "ringmasters"

Pulling all the strings, building,

and running of civilization.

Then there are the "acrobats"
like the equilibrists or trapezists
that defy gravity
and perform jaw-dropping pirouettes
as part of their daily lives.

There are as well the "magicians" and "illusionists"
who make us believe,
in what is apparently not real
through their ability
to dream, visualize,
enhance or augment mundane reality,
and some of them actually dare to
and make it a true reality,
causing incremental quantum leaps
for the advancement and evolution of society.
Then, there the "jugglers"
who master dexterity and multi-tasking,
as if it was second nature to them,
in order not only
to meet the challenges of a complex world
but more importantly,
to be the ones who
assemble, operate,
and maintain

"the engines of civilization."

There are "the lion and tiger tamers"
that control the rule-breakers,
the wild and uncivilized,
maintaining social order and peace,
through the enforcement
of the laws of men.
Then, there are the "sword swallowers"
and "fire eaters"
who defy danger and death
with each and every move or throw;
we usually hand them the controls
and put out lives in their hands
because we trust their skills
as well as their endless rehearsal and preparation,
to deliver us safely to our destination;
as their feats don't allow
for a single false step or bad move.
Then, there are the "cannonball men"
who like to live on a bang;
for them, the flights to nowhere
are the high they need and seek,
and, for these flights,
they are willing to take life to the limit,

just to fly for a few seconds,

even though their trajectory

inevitably always ends,

in a crash and burn situation.

Then, there are the "clowns and jesters"

always after a practical joke or a roast,

whether through ridicule,

outrageousness or burlesque;

They are perennially chasing

The lighter side of things,

in pursuit of laughter or a smile,

which there are never enough in life.

Then there are the "spectators and patrons"

who witness, and approve or disapprove

of everything that takes place

in the show in a ring;

they are demanding and judgmental;

and as an intelligent herd,

they never miss a beat

and sometimes even alter,

the very acts of life in a circus.

Same as children never forget

their first time at the circus,

the biggest show on Earth,

appeals to the inner child

in all of us as well;

and this occurs because in a circus

we witness the show of life

without prejudice,

social rules, filters,

or the arrest of the mundane.

The circus' spectacle displays performers

in the exercise of their best talents,

candidly exposed,

in executing stunning acts,

that even though rehearsed to perfection,

are so daring and outrageous,

even seemingly impossible,

that we rave in childlike exuberance.

As we do in life,

circus performers

come from all walks of life,

but they all have something in common,

spectators recognize and covet;

they do what they love

and what they are passionate about.

Circus performers achieve their high standards

through exceptional drive and desire,

innate abilities, and strenuous preparation

over extended periods of time.

We find circus performers,

on every corner of the streets of life,

not only as shiny artists and elite athletes,

but also, as common citizens,

willing to tap their full potential

by pursuing what they are good at.

We all have a bit or much

of these characters inside each one of us.

What is it?

A bit of a clown and a full-blown illusionist?

Or a bit of a trapezist and a full-blown juggler?

Or perhaps a bit of a ringmaster

and a full-blown clown?

Whoever is the circus character that fits us best,

fact is,

that in the characters of a circus reside

some of our best talents and strengths.

On the characters of a circus,

we get to contemplate and appreciate

what happens?

When we tap our full potential.

Life is a circus,

in as much as,

we let out inner child rejoice and embrace

its own characters,

without filters, fears, or prejudice;

in order to discover which one

or several of them is us,

so we can unleash and soar

with the best use of our talents and passions,

like true circus performers do.

As Mr. Lafayette finishes, he gazes in joy at the sight of Victoria and Erasmus with their eyes wide open and mesmerized expressions of awe and wonder for the power and richness of the poem they've just heard. But, Mr. L is not done yet.

"Most, if not all of the characters in a circus inhabit each one of us. At a minimum, we have a bit of each one of them inside. But for some, we were literally born as one of the circus performers. The challenge then is, what are we? A ringmaster or an equilibrist? A trapezist or a juggler? A clown or a magician? Finding this out and mastering it holds the key for a good performance in the circus of life," concludes the wise antiquarian.

"Do we choose who we want to be in life?" asks a pensive Erasmus.

"To a degree yes, but to a degree no, as we're born with a series of aptitudes that prescribe what we should aim to master. You'll never be a trapezist in a circus simply because you want to. You'll be one if you have a natural ability coupled with a strong

215

desire and an intense and continuous effort to master it. Given those three premises, in the end, you will be a proficient trapezist," adds Mr. L.

"Why compare life to a circus?" asks a perplexed Victoria.

"To contemplate life as a circus is an exercise in wisdom. On one side, life's circumstances present themselves pretty much in the same way all of these characters in the circus do, when they perform for us. On the other hand, the extreme activities and planned mayhem in the three rings in a tent, symbolize at the same time, hard-earned virtuosity and masterfully executed talent. To perfect one or several of the characters of a circus is to master life when it comes to similar circumstances. After all, it cannot escape any of us, that plenty of our lives' feats are pure and simply acts of magic or balance, juggling or taming, acrobatics or clowning, ring mastering or even simply those of being patrons."

Royal Cambridge Scholastic Institute (2019)
(University's Auditorium)

Professor Cromwell-Smith brings everyone back with a clownish smile.

"Try to identify within yourself each of the characters of a circus, whether an acrobat or a juggler or a clown? Then try to find which one is the prevalence in you. Which one are you inclined to be the best at?" concludes Professor Cromwell-Smith acting as a ringmaster.

"See you all next week."

The eminent professor leaves while seemingly immersed in deep thoughts. He wonders which of the circus characters lives within himself.

CHAPTER 12

CLARITY IN LIFE

Royal Cambridge Scholastic Institute (2019)
(Erasmus and Victoria's Campus Home)

As Erasmus enters his cozy home studio in pre-dawn darkness, a lingering thought comes back, 'she's not aware of her worst fears and conceals her propensity for sorrowfulness.' The pot of tea and biscuits lying atop the reading lamp table is a surprise and makes him feel loved. The small note on the side lightens him even more.

"Love you, always have, always will."

Erasmus ruminates for what seems like an eternity and only snaps back when he hears the voice in the background. Then both her arms wrap around him.

"Dear lady of the night, what a delightful pleasure to have you here this early."

"You were in a trance. A deep, deep one," she whispers, still half asleep.

"You make me so happy dear. I only wish we wouldn't have lost so much time apart," she laments.

'Here we go,' reasons a perceptive Erasmus.

"Why would you wish that?" he asks pressing.

"Because sometimes I wish I could reverse time so we could go back and prevent our forty years of separation."

Before uttering a single additional word, Erasmus decides to let her vent everything she has inside.

"I can't help it and constantly fall into this endless loop of pain that I can't, or sometimes it seems, don't want to get out from – like our separation, David's sickness and death, and my interrupted criminal psychology career," she says full of regret and sorrow.

"Dear, there is something very important I have to tell you. It's about a conversation I had with Gina back then. It took place right after my parents came to visit me in Boston."

"You mean the time that you didn't introduce me to your old folks?" Erasmus recalls while prudence dictates restraint and silence as he continues listening to her.

"This is a transcendental anecdote … I've always obsessed about it, replicating it endlessly inside of my head … Let me take you there …," Victoria announces without asking whether he is up to it or not.

Harvard (1977)
(Gina's Dorm Room)

"Are you getting cold feet?" asks Gina.

An uneasy silence comes between the two close friends and former roommates, 'til Victoria starts to mumble a few words.

"A teacher, is that all he's ever going to be?" Victoria asks thinking aloud.

"Vicky, is success-driven love all you care about?" Gina poignantly asks.

"Sometimes it feels like it," she babbles back.

"You know what I think. That's just your excuse - the argument about success and wealth is not yours. When you talk like this, all you're doing is repeating what you've heard all of your life – from your mom. But, the Victoria I know doesn't really care about material things," Gina states with her usual bluntness.

Vicky stays quiet but her eyes are filled with anxiety and fear.

"No Victoria, what you worry about is whether the absent-minded intellectual Brit will take care of you in the way they taught you at home," Gina continues.

"I don't need anyone to take care of me!" Vicky snaps back.

"Yes, you do. You want to be tended! You want to be in control but you want to be tended," Gina states back.

"What's wrong with that?" Victoria asks finally being sincere with herself.

"That's not going to work with Erasmus and his British working ethic. He's in love with an independent and hard-working woman that provides for herself," states Gina.

It all feels utterly crude and uncomfortable to Victoria - but Gina is not done.

"Further Vicky, unless you resolve your acute self-esteem issues with this guy, you'll be under pressure all your life to keep up with his world. Sometimes I feel that what really drives your insecurities and desire to run away and marry whom your mom wants, is that deep inside, you feel totally and terribly inadequate in relation to him. You're not afraid of him. You're afraid of him leaving you. You wrongly believe there is a significant and insurmountable intellectual disadvantage between you and the man who is the love of your life. For that reason, you believe that the relationship is not going to work out. But Vicky, these are only mind games taking place in your confused head. I think Erasmus has brought out of you an independent, confident, genuine, unmaterialistic and wholehearted Victoria. The best of you is out Vicky. Put this thought in your head and remind yourself relentlessly about it – he loves you the way you are, not the way your parents and society want you to be," Gina concludes.

Royal Cambridge Scholastic Institute (2019)
(Erasmus and Victoria's Campus Home)

"I should have listened to her, but I didn't dear," Victoria laments.

"Vicky on the issues of lingering regrets and laments about the past, do you recall when we sat with Mrs. Peabody and she presented us with that magnificent old scribble about regrets and sorrows?"

"Of course I do dear. Why?" she replies and asks defensively but already sensing where he's going.

"Today in class, we'll revisit that day and you know what, I am convinced it will be helpful for you if you would join me."

"With pleasure, dear," she uncomfortably states.

"It'll be quite fitting indeed my lady," he says with a broad smile. Within half an hour they drive to his class in silence. He's cheerful and relieved and she, on the other hand, is pensive and morose. Nevertheless, the couple holds hands throughout the short ride. It is a tight grip of reassurance and strength as if both want to capture and preserve love forever.

Royal Cambridge Scholastic Institute (2019)
(University's Auditorium)

"How's everyone today?"

"Insanely awesome, professor!"

"As you may have noticed, Victoria has joined us today as well and there is a good reason for it. We will visit one of Victoria and my most memorable days indeed. It begins like this ..."

Massachusetts Coast (1977)
(Sailing)

Erasmus isn't much of a sailor but Vicky is. Since an early age, on her summer family vacations on Lake Michigan, her father took her out sailing for hours and hours. Today, they have rented a small sailing boat, and starting in Newburyport, the two youngsters have sailed out into the Atlantic Ocean along Salisbury Beach. Staying close to shore, they have headed south as Vicky teaches Erasmus all the basic sailing elements,

223

including its navigating equipment and the wind. Once she's confident that he is proficient enough to share control of the boat, the two youngsters let themselves go. Soon after, the elements and the landscape take over. The would-be sailors have just become spectators. The scene has become a magnificent display of nature's wonders. The breeze carries them along the coast and the sounds of the sea inexorably engulf them. That's when, inspired and without notice, the young poet starts to recite rhymed words of art to Vicky in verses that are quickly swept away by the wind, but not before they are engraved on her heart. Let's call it …

"Those Shiny Curls of Mine"

The gentle breeze tussles freely,

those shiny curls of mine.

The vast ocean reflects

a magnificent canvas

to draw into eternity,

those incandescent eyes

that I belong to,

now and forever.

With a cornucopia

of blues, silver, and whites,

I am handed the privilege

of an endless palette,

to paint your gorgeous smile

that now owns me whole,

with no room to spare,

but just for our two big hearts,

tightly bundled together,

loving each other to no end.

On one side of the horizon,

the sun rises

bringing soft, bright hues of light

to the new day,

and along with it,

an aura of ethereal beauty

to your morning self,

one I contemplate in awe and wonder

and wish it to be as well, only mine.

Simultaneously,

on the other side of the horizon,

the sun sets

with intense tones,

same as your passions and fires,

to those, I surrender forever,

through them, my heart is completely yours

and no longer mine.

And in the middle of the horizon

as a backdrop to

our sails and craft,

displaying every color

there is in our universe,

sits an extraordinary

rainbow traversing the skies in full,

from end to end,

framing you at the center

and into a perennial pose,

with your gorgeous smile,

incandescent eyes

and the gentle sea breeze

tussling freely

those beautiful, shining, curls of mine.

Victoria sits still, paying attention to nothing else but him. Her lower lip trembles ever so slightly. Her eyes are transfixed and her facial gesture is one of absolute infatuation over his magical verse and words. It is only after a few minutes that their conversation turns mundane once more.

"What's the name of that tip of land?" he asks.

"Cape Ann and slightly to the right you can see Halibut Point," she replies.

"Is that where we're going?" he asks as this is her trek and her route.

"Actually no, we're heading towards that small bay closer to us to the right, it's called Ipswich Bay," she answers while pointing it out to him.

"Why is it called that?" asks an incredulous Erasmus.

"You silly, don't you know? It's the bay of the famous Ipswich clams," she declares, happy to know something he doesn't for a change.

"Is that our final destination?" he quizzes pressing the point.

"No, that's a surprise dear," she says in mystery.

With a smooth breeze on their backs, they sail up the coast. Victoria deftly maneuvers the wind until they approach the picturesque harbor where they find an empty dock. Erasmus helps by tying their sailboat to the minuscule wooden structure.

Lanesville, Mass. Coast Line (1977)

Once they come ashore, after a scenic and distended stroll, Erasmus realizes that they're in Lanesville, their beloved antiquarian, Mrs. Peabody's lair. They walk a short distance and see their beloved mentor's storefront. As soon as they enter, their effusive host quickly approaches them with open arms.

"Mrs. P," Erasmus states smiling.

"Well, well, well this is a surprise," she says in high spirits.

Mrs. Peabody bear hugs both of them in an embrace for two.

"Before I forget Erasmus, back in Wales you have a melancholic fan of yours howling abandonment," she lovingly scolds him.

"Young Erasmus, you haven't written to her in more than a year," Mrs. P continues, now deadly serious.

"Mrs. V?" asks Vicky.

"The one and only," replies Mrs. P with an admonishing look all over her face.

But it's only a façade that doesn't last long with the effusive antiquarian host, especially after Erasmus promises and promises to write to his beloved mentor as soon as he gets back home.

"Mrs. P, we need a remedy for the soul," he suggests.

"Ajah, that's a transcendental matter that requires further clarification," Mrs. P says.

"What is the affliction if I may ask?" Mrs. P questions.

"Well, it's about regrets and sorrows. I'm always hung up on both of them," states Erasmus in embarrassment.

"Mrs. P, make it a strong remedy please. He badly needs it," requests Victoria in earnest.

Mrs. Peabody is already on the move before Vicky even ends her request. It takes just a few minutes, but inexplicably at least to the naked eye, she manages to find the book from one of the piles within the chaos around her.

"This is one of my favorite readings, ever since I lost my husband to the sea, during a fateful storm off the New England coast," the loving mentor explains to the surprise of the youngsters who were totally ignorant about her loss.

228

Mrs. P then places the scribble on her converted dining table and starts to read with a teary-eyed face.

"Clarity in Life"

Those that regret in never-ending fashion,

those that drown in their sorrows

seemingly forever,

lack clarity in life.

Craving for an alternative reality

of "what ifs" what could have or should have been

is a fruitless search,

for a time machine,

an alternative reality or dimension

that simply do not exist.

Lamenting past events, difficulties, even tragedies

on endless loops of pain,

leaves us stuck, infinitely gasping for air.

Regrets and sorrows are fueled and driven

by deeply ingrained insecurities, fear, and guilt;

All of them working as magnifying glasses

distorting and exaggerating true pain and real losses.

Regrets and sorrows take us to places

where we end up with those we don't like or love,

doing what we don't want,

longing for people, things

we no longer have or never did,

or simply are not present any longer.

Material wealth allows freedom from poverty

but it is not a substitute for fear, guilt,

shortcomings, false aspirations,

or the void of emptiness of spirit and soul.

Riches are not only existentially worthless

misleading us into a false sense of security;

they are also another murky, existential source,

forming future states of loneliness, regret and sorrow.

We achieve clarity in life,

when we have a clear purpose,

constantly focusing on our search for meaning.

We achieve clarity in life,

when we are fully aware

of our strengths and weaknesses,

when we constantly and relentlessly,

seek to build a wholesome set of virtues,

and we are fully aware of which of those virtues

we have already acquired,

then strive to put them into action.

We achieve clarity in life

when we conduct ourselves with responsibility,

while exercising judicious discipline.

We achieve clarity in life

when we invariably seek, accept,

defend and protect the truth.

When we achieve clarity in life,

we are graced with redemption for our fallings,

through the power of our faith and beliefs,

under the mantle of trust.

We achieve clarity in life when we understand

that we can always reinvent ourselves;

moving forward without breaking our core,

following our convictions with unyielding fashion

and treasuring true love,

using it as our source of happiness and inspiration.

Clarity in life inexorably leads

to accomplishment and self-confidence,

which in turn lead us to virtuous circles,

where regrets and sorrows have no place to be,

nor any air to breath.

Clarity in life opens life for us,

expanding our horizons,

leaving no sky limits before us,

just the living-universe and its endless firmament

for us to experience, enjoy and appreciate.

Mrs. Peabody closes the book in a rather solemn fashion. She contemplates the young couple with doting and pensive eyes.

"Victoria and Erasmus, life is always in constant motion; lingering negatives are simply incompatible with the dynamics of being truly alive."

Royal Cambridge Scholastic Institute (2019)
(University's Auditorium)

Professor Cromwell-Smith brings his class back by adding to the same thought.

"Ever since that day, I never again got trapped in those recurring painful thoughts," he says.

Victoria is staring at him with a face of regret and embarrassment. "Thank you," she says with her lips wearing an expression of realization.

Erasmus tips his head in acknowledgment but still remains solemn with a rictus that seems to signal - enough Vicky.

But, the class is not over yet.

"Professor, what about when the loss is irreplaceable?" asks a young Hispanic student.

"In Korean culture, they define certain kinds of pain as unresolved sorrows. This philosophy is known as Han. There are losses and tragedies that we acknowledge and accept. We don't hide, ignore or try to avoid them. To the contrary, we recognize their existence and have to face the fact that they're not going away. We're aware that the pain will subsist. But we don't allow them to control or drive our lives, as we put them in their proper place," Cromwell-Smith replies in wisdom.

"Professor, what to do when regrets or sorrows want to take a hold of you?" asks a tall and lanky student with a southern accent.

"Something that I learned from my mother and I've done since I was a young teenager," the professor replies and then adds, "when you feel it coming, or when you realize that you've fallen in any of those states, first of all, breathe slowly and deeply, and as you inhale, spell the word LIFE in your mind. Then, breathe and say LIFE while visualizing the word spreading all over you. Repeat it until the angst subsides. It works wonders," the professor states.

"That'll be all for today, see you all next week," he says parting ways.

Then as the professor and Victoria leave, they see many of the students breathing deeply and in resolute calmness.

"They seem to be at peace dear, perhaps now it's me who'll quit regretting and lamenting for good, as you did way back then," she says with resolve.

"I'm sure you will my lady, I'm sure you will," he says with caution, but wanting to believe her with all his heart.

Victoria remains pensive while walking alongside Erasmus. They hold interlocking hands as they always do. Her tight grip enables Erasmus to sense the energy boiling inside of her.

"Dear, coming with you today to class has helped me a great deal to bring clarity to my unresolved sorrows," she suddenly says as they sit on a bench at the campus's immaculate park.

"How so my lady?" he cautiously asks.

"It's true, there are things that I'll regret forever, pain that will never go away, and losses that are irreplaceable. But now I know, that I can put them in their proper place and continue to live my life." She reflects aloud as he just listens attentively and in delight, with no desire to interrupt the flow of her reasoning.

"Today, remembering the memorable occasion with Mrs. Peabody has made me realize, that besides lamenting, I have also been acting constructively, but inadvertently, with my own unresolved sorrows," she says thinking aloud in realization.

"Even though I've regretted it forever, not following Gina's advice on that memorable conversation about you, this time, I've not made the same mistake. To the contrary, I've kept her words of wisdom present from the very first day we were reunited," Victoria declares, as she continues her monologue, seemingly seeking reaffirmation within herself.

"Erasmus, the day I went to look for you, I sat in your class, following my daughter's strict instructions not to interrupt you. I waited to announce myself until the very end of the session. After Sarah had done the introduction, I was not only consumed by nerves as I gazed at you from afar but also part of me didn't know if you would take me back," Vicky reveals, piquing Erasmus' interest even further.

"Dear, while I was sitting up in the audience waiting for Sarah to introduce me, I realized that the first mistake I wasn't going to make, was to confuse you wanting me back as an act of weakness on your part. I thought, 'if you would want me back, it would only be out of the sheer strength of your character,' it would mean that you would have already seen through the façade of me leaving you and would have already forgiven me. So, the challenge in fact was only about me and whether I'd been honest and had forgiven myself. Accepting me back didn't mean we will last either, because even though our affinity and friendship would pick up right where we left off, our passionate love would be a totally different matter. Lust would require mutual desire."

"Erasmus, you love self-sufficient, non-controlling, passionate women. I on the other hand, was coming from a relationship where I could do anything I wanted with my husband and I quickly realized, that wasn't going to work with you for even one minute."

"I recall while watching you address your class, that the intense attraction I always had for you came from the fact that I was hardly ever able to control or manipulate you. Additionally, in relation to love and romance, you are filled with reciprocate ingenuity, candor, and innocence, meaning that you would never accept anything less and would spot how I really felt rather quickly. That made me understand that I had to leave my brain out of the equation from the get-go. In that regard, my problem was even bigger as I was coming from a relationship where I dealt with my then husband in purely rational terms in a controlled manner. I reminded myself, that such behavior was not only a non-starter with you but also a recipe for total disaster. So, I made the adjustments dear. Starting right there, before I even called your name, I was dealing with my regrets, guilt, and sorrows. I wanted to open up to you with the honest truth."

"We've been working things out together. And, as far as friendship, passion, and love goes, I have just let my heart drive me. This has enabled me to be myself, the same person you knew when we were students at Harvard," Victoria concludes with clear eyes and an open heart.

Overcome by emotion, Erasmus stops and puts both palms of his hands around Vicky's face, and kisses her with passion and gratitude. Vicky embraces him even tighter than ever as if trying to make him hers forever.

CHAPTER 13

GRATITUDE

Royal Cambridge Scholastic Institute (2019)
(Erasmus and Victoria Campus's Home)

The professor paces as he reads a voluminous book in his home studio. It is still dark and in the early hours of the morning when Erasmus is surprised by Victoria. As it is her custom, she approaches him from behind and slides her arms around him running her fingers underneath his robe and around his chest as she whispers in his ear … "I love you."

"Me too my lady," he replies dropping the book on his desk and placing his hands over hers, while she is still caressing his torso.

"What a pleasure it is to see you at this early hour of the morning," he continues.

"Well, yesterday when you were staring at me in a way you'd never done before, I asked you what it was that you were staring at. You replied that you simply like to stare endlessly at my face. When I asked you why once more, you replied that in order to respond and explain it well enough, you were going to write me something about it," she says in the form of a lead-off statement.

"And my lady believes that somehow I've already tackled and completed such a worthy but challenging endeavor?" he asks,

237

teasing her and slowly turning around while her cozy embrace continues making it hard to concentrate.

"Knowing you, I'm certain you already did," she affirms with absolute self-confidence.

Erasmus is now staring at her every facial gesture and movement. Seemingly, once more he gets quickly lost.

"Erasmus dear, come back to earth please," she lovingly pleads trying to draw his attention.

A faint smile forms on Erasmus' happy face. Without breaking their embrace, he reaches and picks up a small scroll from on top of his desk. It is tied up with a tiny string and an impossibly cute knot.

"Go ahead open it, I planned to give it to you later this morning after you woke up, but I underestimated your ineffable curiosity."

She opens it with a big smile on her face.

"Please read it to me dear," she pleads. Erasmus starts to read in earnest …

"Contemplating Your Face"

Over time our faces become a reflection of our lives

and what we are comprised of inside.

Over time the mask of youth fades away

as we bear the marks and scars

of the kind and way of life

we have lived or experienced it.

Like a fingerprint,

in a well weathered face,

every little crevice, corner, ridge, or wrinkle

coming out of our unguarded rictuses

and spontaneous gestures,

reflect our deeds,

our highs, lows,

wins, losses, and defeats,

our pain and joy –

in plain sight and exposed for all to see,

like signage there is nothing

we can do to hide them.

Does our face look deeply angry?

What about mean-spirited?

Perhaps artificial?

Or does it exude goodness, nobility,

a gentle spirit, and an inspired soul?

Does it show darkness and solitude?

Or optimism and enthusiasm?

Does it vibe anguish perhaps sadness?

Or does it reflect happiness?

Does it show depression and despair?

Or cheerfulness and passion?

Whatever your honest answer is,

that's likely who you really are.

But nothing in our face conveys more

about our true nature and human condition

than our eyes.

There are those that are downright scary

as they portray death in those that have been

in contact with it,

for the right or wrong reasons.

Others depict madness

and we can sense the tumultuous,

unsettled internal world of the person we face.

What about those that are simply empty

and there is no one home?

There is an endless gallery in display

throughout the human species –

the envious eyes,

the obsessed,

the ambitious,

the vengeful,

the sad,

the angry,

the resentful,

the greedy,

and the hypocrite.

These contrast with those that are

gentle,

benign,

giving,

doting,

inspiring,

healing,

happy,

joyful,

patient,

grateful,

forgiving,

or simply,

twinkling,

or even magical

and outright awesome!

Then there is love.

Our eyes and faces are transformed

under the mantle of love;

Youth, freshness, rosiness, sparkle, and glow

and cover us with a halo

that projects positive energy

impregnated with enchanting

and contagious vitality.

The look of love is a masterpiece,

where we see drawn on our loved ones

all that we share and treasure with them.

That's why,

when we contemplate the faces of our life partners,

we see well beyond what anyone else does

as every move and every angle

reflects a different moment of a life shared.

Each expression and gesture

remind us of a different anecdote,

or circumstance or life experience with them.

We place their laughter on eternal memories,

we vividly remember their smiles

at countless occasions and places

awe see their tears of joy or sadness

as those we shared or experienced as a couple.

We see in flashes drawn on their faces

the movie of our life journey,

just like the first time we discovered

our love's maternal or paternal eyes

at our children's births,

or their eyes of sadness on each of our departures

followed by their bursts of joy and relief

upon our safe returns,

or their gestures of disgust

at our transgressions or disappointments,

or their immense happiness

when their heart was taken

by surprise by spontaneous gestures,

heartfelt little details or even a tiny single flower.

When we see that face

that has journeyed with us for so long,

we see every little thing, wear and tear

that is as much a part of us as it is of them.

That's how we can't help but to contemplate,

unwittingly and to a degree unknowingly,

in awe and wonder

the unique kind of beauty

that is made out of the richness of a joined life story

filled with countless and unforgettable mementos.

That is the reason

no one can appreciate and value,

understand, read, see and feel better

our life's partners eyes and faces than us,

simply because only we have experienced and know

the life story and anecdotes behind them.

As he finishes reading, her eyes are lost in a sea of emotions. "You never cease to amaze me my beloved Brit. Sometimes you are simply, enchanting and spellbinding. There is profound beauty and addictive wizardry in your words, my love," she professes to him with a stare that denotes immense gratitude. Slowly her gaze starts to change from an enamored look into a wicked one filled with tease. She approaches him deliberately and kisses him with passion and then extends her arms and takes his hand. Victoria draws him upstairs with intensity and they quickly become immersed in their never-ending lovemaking crusade.

(Victoria and Erasmus's Campus Home)

A couple of hours later, the sun is just breaking as Ella Fitzgerald and Louis Armstrong's "Our Love is Here to Stay" plays in the background. Sipping her morning coffee, Victoria looks through the window as the sound "extraordinaire" fills the air.

Far away in the distance, the figure of Erasmus on his way to class slowly shrinks away as he bikes through the tree-lined road. As the music beat goes on at full blast, one of her favorite tunes, Laura Pausini's "Amare Veramente" (true loving) inundates the space and she quickly gets lost inside the paths of her joyful heart.

'The well-hidden loneliness is gone, the chronic melancholy has vanished. Work is no longer an evasion tool but simply passion and pleasure, and strangely enough, I feel protected,' she reflects in peace.

Erasmus is now simply but a tiny dot ready to be swallowed by the distant hill. Then as if dropping down, he disappears. The slight jolt of fear she feels is an instinctive reaction of her adaptive subconscious to the awkward fading away of her loved one. She tries to rationalize that he has just gone over the top of the hill, but her gut feeling starts to grow. Is she imagining things? Ominously Judy Garland's "Stormy Weather" starts to play. Is it just her mind playing games?

247

'Perhaps I should get on the bike and go and take a look,' she reasons, while urging herself – and that she does. Within seconds, untied bathrobe and all, she storms out of the house and pedals in angst.

Then, the faint sound of a siren makes her cringe. The next seconds seem like an eternity as the emergency alarm sound keeps on increasing in volume until the confirmation that likely something has happened, as the ambulance speeds by her on the way up the hill.

Shortly after, out of breath, Victoria reaches the top. The first thing she sees is that of a campus security car and an officer holding Erasmus' head. The paramedics are lowering a stretcher. When she reaches him, his eyes are closed. "Nooo!" she exclaims in fear.

Then, on an impulse she lurches forward, and kneeling on the ground she places both hands on his face.

"Erasmus dear," she pleads in anguish.

"Ma'am, move over please, let us do our job," commands one of the paramedics.

But she doesn't move and as tears cascade down her face, she continues to caress his cheeks and forehead. Then, as she's about to be removed, all of a sudden his eyes open up and his first sight is of her.

"Victoria," he blurts with a faint smile on his face. Her sobs quickly morph into a teary smile of deep relief and lots of heavy breathing.

"What happened my lady?" he asks seemingly clueless.

"I thought I saw you falling in the distance and out of a premonition made my way over here."

"I was driving in the opposite direction and suddenly he sort of hit something, lost control and veered towards me. I slammed on the brakes but he still landed on his chest with his arms extended over the hood of my patrol car," states the campus security guard.

"Actually, that may have broken the fall and averted a possible head-on concussion," states one of the paramedics as he and his colleague load Erasmus onto the stretcher.

"I hit a pothole and lost my balance," Erasmus suddenly blurts out recalling what actually happened.

After thirty minutes of back and forth, Erasmus insists on staying with Vicky and as the ambulance and campus patrol car leaves, the grateful and relieved couple stands alone at the top of the same eventful hill.

"Dear, I'm so grateful nothing happened to you. When I first saw you, lying on the ground with your eyes shut, for an instant I thought I'd lost you," she says holding tight to him.

"Dear, this is one of those moments when we show gratitude, don't you think?" she says winking at him.

"Do you remember the first time we did this?" asks Victoria as she places her hand on his heart and brings his to hers.

"Close your eyes," she whispers.

Then, staring at him with intense faith, she professes.

"Being alive and having you are precious and irreplaceable gifts, I have to earn every day. Let us thank the creator. Let us thank life." They both recite in unison.

Then, as Erasmus opens his eyes, the first sight is the reassuring stare of his other half.

"Of course, Victoria, how could I ever forget it," he replies with a broad smile.

"You still have time," she says casually on the surface, but with clear intent underneath.

"For what?" he asks with his usual cluelessness.

"To make gratitude the subject of today's class," she responds with a leading remark.

"Do I?"

"You still have an hour. Let's go back and you can take a shower," she volunteers with a wink that quickly snares him completely.

"What a wonderful idea. It's a keeper. Right. My lady, it'll be a pleasure to pedal with you back to the house," he says as the awkward twosome makes their way back home, zigzagging, through the gentle downhill, Erasmus on his old rusty bike and Victoria on her more modern two-wheeler.

Royal Cambridge Scholastic Institute (2019)
(University's Auditorium)

"How's everyone today?" asks an inspired professor, hardly being able to hide his joy from his recent bath of passion.

"Awesome professor!" replies a spirited student body.

The buzz and energy in the room are palpable to everyone.

"Today, I'll be revisiting a day I will remember forever, as I hope it'll be for you as well. It begins like this …"

New York City, Carnegie Hall (1977)

Being invited over by the Scottish antiquarian, Colin Carnegie, who is on a short visit to the USA, Victoria and Erasmus travel overnight by train from Boston to New York City. After a day in the city's parks, museums, and public libraries, in excitement and in their best "attires", they attend a night gala concerto. It's their first time at Carnegie Hall. And it turns out to be a memorable experience as rock genius, Rick Wakeman, takes them on a "Journey to the Center of the Earth." Then as they exit, Mr. Carnegie is waiting for them.

"Victoria, Erasmus, what a pleasure it is to see you both in here. I'm so happy you could make it. But tell me, how was it?" he babbles nonstop in excitement.

"Fantastic, I read all of the Jules Verne's books when I was a child. But, I would've never imagined that I would get to experience that particular book 'Journey To The Center Of The

Earth' in a rock concert, much less with a philharmonic orchestra in the background," states an exuberant Erasmus.

"Mr. Carnegie, I assume this magnificent hall is also part of your relative's legacy," Erasmus asks.

"That's right," he replies with pride.

"As you said, the magnificent deeds he left, not only continue to exist and operate but have also become weaved into the fabric of this country," states Erasmus with pride.

"Well said young man. Well said. It has become like the air we breathe. First of all, we're not that aware that we have it. We just use and enjoy it. It's the same with the man himself, Andrew Carnegie. His foundation, in real dollar terms, meaning adjusted by inflation, is the largest philanthropic organization ever created, but that's not that well known in the country," he states in acclamation.

"A true measure of the stature of the man himself," states Erasmus.

"But as you have said, he's not appreciated enough," states Victoria.

"That's right," acknowledges Mr. Carnegie.

"Why is that?" she asks in exuberant naiveté.

"That, I'll leave for you to discover. It is a worthy endeavor, though. I sincerely hope that America at some point in time, recognizes and acclaims commensurately, the great deeds of the man."

"Gratitude?" asks Victoria.

"Indeed, young lady. His legacy has earned it in spades," states Mr. C, continuing.

"Let's have a seat. On the subject of gratitude, I've brought with me an ancient writing, so our encounter doesn't elapse without a measure of tutelage for you both," their doting tutor states as they make themselves comfortable on a Carnegie Hall pew. Then, the Scottish antiquarian starts to read in earnest.

"Gratitude"

The most important forms of Gratitude

are either celestial or existential in nature.

Enough has been professed and predicated, describing

Gratitude.

Yet, its essence does not lie in the

WHAT IS IT?

It resides in the WHEN, WHY, AND HOW.

We are truly grateful when we are Selfless in our gestures and

expectations.

We are genuinely grateful on our actions

if we are keenly Aware of its existential

and imperative necessity;

such, to perennially reciprocate

and give back to life and others,

for the privilege of being alive.

For Gratitude to be authentically proffered

or conveyed;

for Gratitude to resonate or be empathetic;

It requires the virtues of Humility and Respect.

Selflessness, Awareness, Humility, And Respect

Are the essence of WHEN, WHY AND HOW Gratitude

takes place.

Our mere existence is inexplicably fortunate,

immensely blessed;

And for it, we thank our Creator for ordaining us

into this universe,

instead of the trillions of other reproductive cells,

that never make it through

the procreation and gestation stages,

preceding birth.

Once we arrive, though,

we have much to be thankful for,

certainly for every day

we are alive, healthy, conscious,

and surrounded by friends and family;

but alongside these two is our Gratitude for others.

In Gratitude,

We recognize the loyalty others demonstrate to us.

In Gratitude,

We value the faith others maintain in us.

In Gratitude,

We acknowledge the worthiness

of one another's gestures.

In Gratitude,

We pay our respects as human beings

to those that dote on us whether we deserve it or not.

In Gratitude,

We reattribute with love, the love received.

In Gratitude,

We reward the acts of kindness we are graced with.

In Gratitude,

We enjoy what we give far more

than what we receive.

In Gratitude,

We celebrate the naive and candid side of life.

Gratitude is most impactful

when it genuinely comes from the heart,

without the interference of ego or social rules.

Genuine Gratitude does not expect anything

in return.

Genuine Gratitude is spontaneous,

not dictated by anything or anyone.

Genuine Gratitude is anonymous

and it is just an act of our conscience.

Genuine Gratitude uplifts

who or what we are grateful for, first,

at the forefront,

while we remain behind the scenes.

Genuine Gratitude is never

proportionate or measurable in magnitudes.

Genuine Gratitude is expressed

through acts of love, gestures, and even sacrifices.

To the contrary, false Gratitude is a narcissistic farce,

as our only real concern is ourselves and our image,

not anyone else's.

Gratitude is a dependable source

of inner peace, happiness and inspiration,

as its musical notes sing

to the better side of our human condition,

where the spark of creativity and visualization

can be ignited in an instant,

triggering one of the noblest of all conditions,

that of being perennially thankful

to the Creator, for life, and to others.

Colin Carnegie stares at them with a big smile.

"Now, let me share with you an exercise in gratitude. One that hopefully you'll apply for the rest of your lives," states Mr. Carnegie.

Royal Cambridge Scholastic Institute (2019)
(University's Auditorium)

Professor Cromwell-Smith brings back everyone to the present in order to demonstrate what the Scottish antiquarian taught Vicky and him that day. It is the same exercise Victoria did with Erasmus earlier in the morning at the site of his uneventful but scary mishap.

"Let me show you what Mr. Carnegie asked us to profess that night at Carnegie Hall. It'll be a timeless and invaluable lesson for you all. Here is what I want you to do. Please stand up," he asks them.

The entire student body stands up as requested. The professor then quiets the growing rumble.

"This is what our beloved mentor taught us that day. Place one of your hands over your heart. Now, close your eyes and within your mind, say the following words. 'Being alive and healthy is a precious and irreplaceable gift that I have to earn every day. Let us thank the creator. Let us thank life.'"

The entire auditorium is silent as the act of gratitude takes place.

"See you all next week," states the professor.

Then, as he leaves he can see many of the students repeating the ritual with hands over their hearts. He smiles as he sees a plentitude of faces showing gratitude.

CHAPTER 14

DOUBT

Royal Cambridge Scholastic Institute (2019)
(Erasmus and Victoria Campus's Home)

Erasmus wakes up in a jolt. His first instinct is to check if she is still there or if she was ever by his side to begin with.

'Your deranged mind is driving you crazy,' he mulls over while he caresses her forehead as she sleeps.

'You are poisoned by doubt and do not seem to be able or willing to get out of it.'

Erasmus drags himself out of bed and tumbles his way to the kitchen to fix his morning tea. But, he finds it ready and warm, with a card next to it. It is a poem that reads:

"Always There"

Today my heart looked for you,

and I sighed in joy and relief,

as one more time,

when I needed it,

my dream of you,

was still there.

Somehow, I'd expected it to vanish,

but that's just the other side of me,

the one that tries to keep me grounded,

not letting me go anywhere.

Tonight, I went to bed early

and your dream of me

remained exactly where you left it,

right there.

Tomorrow, I'll be up before dawn

and shortly after,

at sunrise,

our dream will make itself present,

as it always does,

always there.

He smiles in joy as he reads it again.

'You old fool. What is it going to take to let go of your doubts and fears?' he reasons in angry joy.

"Did you like it?" she asks while standing at the door.

Erasmus turns around in slow motion, flashing a splendorous smile.

"I love it my lady," he answers as he walks and embraces her.

"I recently corresponded with good old Mrs. Peabody, and she was so kind to find it for me among her treasure chest of antique book writings," she says still half asleep.

"You're amazing," he whispers in her ear as she trembles.

"Not exactly dear. I just know exactly what you are going through as the same thing happened to me way back then."

"You mean doubts?" he asks.

"Yeah. I was full of doubts and uncertainty, so I ran," she says in guilt.

"We already went through that Vicky. But I do have a question that has been lingering in my head for days. Something completely different," he states.

"About what?" she asks already sensing what it is.

"Before we get to that, I've got a little something here for you," he says as he hands a single piece of paper to her.

"What is it?" she asks while starting to read.

"It is called – A Labor of Love – and I wrote it right after we first met. It was written to the future you. It reflects how I then visualized what you were going to be, do and achieve in your life as a criminal psychologist."

"A Labor of Love"

What a tough job

to have to navigate through

the darkest corners of the minds of others,

but not yourself.

Those paths where the ground is shaky

where the foundations have cracks,

where the earth moves and,

where some of the tracks of life are blurry,

without enough light

and there is no sense of well-being or happiness.

But perhaps there is no tougher job,

than that of dealing with minds,

that not only lacks such meaning and purpose in life,

but are also potentially or inherently,

wicked, devious, reckless, delusional

or simply love themselves so much

that there is no room or care, for anyone else.

What a tough job to do good,

by improving the mindset of others in need.

What an impossible job to do that for those

in need of redemption,

those in need of a second act in life,

those that very few support or believe in.

What a tough job,

what an impossible job.

What a wonderful labor of love,

that's what you'll do,

that's what you will be leaving in your wake,

that's what you would have done!

As Victoria finishes reading, tears cascade down her face. "This is beautiful," she blurts out, overcome by emotion and memories of the past.

"I did exactly that for quite a while," she reminisces while tenderly caressing his face.

"Which takes us to my lingering question – why did you change careers?" asks Erasmus while sipping his morning tea.

"I was wondering when you were going to ask me about that," she replies.

"What happened Victoria?" he presses.

"A patient became obsessed with me. For more than a year he harassed and threatened my late husband and me. It affected the whole family. Law enforcement intervened and a judge slapped a restraining order on him. He was arrested several times, but all to no avail. His obsession and aggressiveness only escalated more."

Victoria's voice breaks. Erasmus reacts by placing his arm around her shoulder. Her head leans over his forearms and she remains motionless for a while, trying to get her composure back.

"It was a traumatic experience for all of us. As a consequence, I was not able to see any patients ever again. In the end, the nightmares only stopped when I quit my practice altogether," she blurts out in deep pain.

"How did you feel about your decision as time went on?" he asks gingerly.

"I really didn't have a chance to do so. My late husband got sick. In the following five years, there was no time left for anything else," she laments.

"What about now? Will you go back to it?" he insists in curiosity.

"No, I'm done with it. For me it's now only about us," she says kissing him softly on the cheek.

"What about you, dear? Why did you change colleges?" she asks back.

"Well, it had nothing to do with the colleges. I asked for a change because of you," he replies at once.

"Me? Why?" asks an incredulous Victoria.

"It was sort of a renewal. I needed to change my life. It was my own little way of moving on," he says.

"Did you?" she asks.

"Yes, the new faculty did wonders for me, but no, I never moved on from us – that never materialized," affirms Erasmus.

"And you my lady, never had any doubts?"

"When I left, I was overtaken by them," she laments.

"I never did," he states with firmness in his voice.

"But why have them now?" she asks trying to make sense.

"That's what I can't figure out, especially their recurring nature," he replies.

"Perhaps what you are, is terrified of me leaving again. There is a part of you that holds fears and doubts about the same thing happening once more. My bet is that it'll go away over time," Victoria diagnoses as the psychologist in her takes over.

"It'll certainly go away at lightning speed, if every time I feel one of these panic attacks building up, you stop me right in my tracks before it even gets going. And you do it so beautifully with all of your expressions and little gestures of unconditional love," he affirms.

"Dear, there are things inside all of us that are better left unexplained – don't try to find an answer for everything. Please read this as it is another one of the scribbles Mrs. P sent us."

"A Good Riddle"

A good riddle is hard to crack.

Inevitably though,

they always have a solution.

Same is for a puzzle or a mystery.

But life is not always a riddle

to be solved,

as its solutions don't come in the

form of passwords,

as more often than not

they are created, or simply

changed, along the way.

Hence, even though life's riddles,

are always there to be solved,

their solutions are not necessarily,

already there.

And if one has to be too careful

about what to ask for,

then some of life's riddles are better

left unresolved.

"Thank you my lady," he says in a pensive manner. "Doubt, that'll be today's subject."

"Oh, Mrs. Pointdexter, the librarian at Harvard," she says immediately.

"You do remember!" he says, validating her reply before continuing.

"How could I forget? If only I would've put into practice what we learned that day," he laments.

"You only have a slight problem my dear," she cautions him.

"And what would that be my lady?" he asks intrigued.

"Have you noticed what time it is?" she blurts out with angst as he glances at the wall clock.

Fifteen minutes until class. It seems impossible at first — to make it on time ...

Royal Cambridge Scholastic Institute (2019)
(University's Auditorium)

But, somehow, five minutes later, Victoria, still in her nightgown, drives the professor in his car to the class. Then, with only a minute to spare, he bolts out of the car.

"Love you my wicked lady," he yells as he runs away.

"Love you too, my lunatic Brit," she replies back with her head out of the window.

As he sprints through the corridors, the auditorium is in suspense as the seconds tick away. Is there going to be a second tardy by the professor? Bets are running. Those betting in favor, support the notion that the professor is still honeymooning. Those betting against, believe that he won't be late because his honeymoon is over.

10, 9, 8, 7, 6, 5, 4, 3 …

"Good morning everyone," an out-of-breath professor announces as he barks into the auditorium. He then stares at the audience for what seems a long time, while he paces and catches his breath. When he feels he has them locked in, he continues.

"Today's subject is doubt," he announces.

"Some of you doubted whether I would make it on time to class today. That's what we all do, harness doubts, all of the time. This morning, I'll be taking you back to the day when Victoria and I met a rather remarkable woman at a timeless athenaeum and she provided us with a memorable lesson about the subject. It begins like this …"

Harvard's Widener Library (1977)

"Nowadays this is the only way to get a hold of you guys," Vicky's best friend, Gina, states with sarcasm.

"You both have become absolute love hermits," complains Erasmus's close friend, Matthew.

"We should all go out," adds Gina.

Distractedly, with a touch of amusement, the infatuated young couple observes their friends' smiles and faces, but no words come out of their mouths.

"I guess that's it. We've lost both of them," states Matthew jokingly in resignation.

"Of course, you haven't. Give us time," Victoria interrupts.

"Erasmus, what about your old mentors back in Wales. Did you forget about them as well?" asks Matthew.

"Sort of. I did manage to write to one of them recently, Mrs. V, but only after a colleague of hers reminded me. I did tell her everything about Vicky and I though," replies Erasmus defensively.

"And?" presses Matthew.

"She did reply a while ago," adds Erasmus.

"It was a wonderful letter and with it, she sent us several old writings. I particularly like the one called, "The Three-Legged Stool," states a spirited Victoria.

"Now, Vic, explain something to me," states Matthew in a conspiracy theory tone.

"And what would that be, Matt?" asks an intrigued Victoria.

"You went all out on a limb at Martha's Vineyard when you covered Erasmus' eyes from behind by surprise, then you guys kissed and the rest is history. But, Gina has told us that you didn't even know he was the one!" states Matthew chuckling.

An unforgettable silence ensues, as Victoria bites her lip and looks at Gina with accusatory eyes.

"That's right, I didn't know. I just followed my heart and I swear to you guys that I didn't enter the restaurant with any plan whatsoever in mind. Everything I did was on impulse. It's simply that when I saw Erasmus, I lost control of myself," blurts an emotional Victoria.

"All those little gestures opened her heart, so that outburst was bound to happen," remarks a clinical Gina.

"Well, prince charming, you obviously won her over with the baton!" announces Gina trying to be nice but still coming across as her usual sarcastic self.

"And you, Victoria, captured his heart with the trip home," states Matthew.

The two infatuated youngsters look at each other with expressions that denote there's nothing they've just heard, that they don't already know in their heart of hearts.

"Hey buddy, time to work," states Matthew to Erasmus breaking the spell."

"Vic, we have work to do, let's go," cautions Gina as both girls move away to another table.

A couple of hours later the love birds are alone again in the cavernous Harvard library.

"Let's go and check out the antique book section," states Erasmus.

Giggling and holding hands the two move around not paying much attention to the rules or the other library dwellers.

"May I help you?" sternly states a rather short and skinny bespectacled woman.

"We are looking for antique books," says Erasmus.

"Those you have to request and then read in a special section."

"Why a special section?" asks Victoria in ignorance.

"Video surveillance ensures that you will treat the books with care," the librarian replies impatiently.

"Now, what are you looking for?" the librarian asks.

"We are looking for ancient writings about doubt," Erasmus answers.

"Any particular period or writer?" the librarian asks.

"We will leave that up to you," Erasmus replies.

"May I ask you, what's the nature of your doubt?" the librarian quizzes the youngsters as she is a bit intrigued.

"Of course you can! Mine is about what to do in life," states Erasmus as he turns to Vicky.

"Mine is about whether I want to study criminal psychology or not," adds Vicky, totally omitting her real and growing doubts.

"Those are pretty conventional doubts at this stage of your lives. Why the interest in antique books?" the librarian asks even more puzzled.

"I grew up surrounded by them in Wales," replies Erasmus.

"Hey, you're the boy from Hay-On-Wye and you're the girl from Waterloo, Illinois," the librarian says in surprise.

"Yes, that's us," replies Erasmus with pride, guessing accurately the tightness of the New England antiquarian librarian community.

"I didn't know you were students at Harvard. I am Felicia Pointdexter."

"Erasmus Cromwell-Smith and Victoria Emerson-Lloyd. Nice to meet you," states a spirited Victoria.

"Alright, I know exactly what to get you. It's timeless and unforgettable," affirms the spirited Mrs. Pointdexter. "It'll provide you with the wisdom you are seeking."

The diminutive librarian is only away for a minute or two when in hurried short steps she returns with a scroll.

"Perhaps it's presumptuous of me, but would you allow me to read it to you?" she asks.

Both youngsters are smiling and quickly glance at each other as they shrug their shoulders in unison.

"It'll be an honor," states Erasmus gallantly.

Mrs. Pointdexter dutifully starts to read in earnest...

"Doubt"

A doubt without trust, method, or purpose

sets us up for recurring anxiety and pain,

unfortunately in vain,

as all of it will go to waste,

when inexorably, we fail.

On these type of vacillations,

when we doubt, we are hiding something,

and doubts are just false shields and excuses

for the real roots and genesis of our behavior;

namely, weakness of character, lack of knowledge,

shortcomings on ability or talent,

lack of preparation or planning,

among others.

These type of indecisiveness,

seeks to justify mediocrity and incompetence

through blame or suspicions of others,

when in all likelihood, all that is wrong,

lies only within ourselves.

These type of hesitations,

are like a deadly poison,

inevitably leading to inaction and paralyzing fear;

as we are increasingly overwhelmed by

uncertainty, skepticism, apprehension

and a nagging lack of confidence

that inexorably leads to errors in judgment.

This is the main reason why these types of doubts

are the telltale of failure.

The antidotes to doubting are, trust, method,

and purpose.

When we doubt and apply trust to it,

we get rid of it, by applying the benefit of the doubt to the

person or situation.

We apply method,

when we are objectively uncertain,

our inclination not to believe can be overruled

by the observation of facts.

When we have uncertainty about beliefs or opinions,

we overcome them by curing

our incomplete knowledge or our lack of evidence.

We apply purpose,

when we are on an emotional overload

and under siege

by avalanches of indecision.

We dissolve and break through them,

if, as we discard the waste,

we can keep our end game in sight

and in case we realize we don't have such,

then we eagerly develop one,

as purpose is the ultimate doubt breaker.

In final analysis, a healthy dose of doubt

is an essential component of a wholesome life.

But it is our challenge, in order to embrace doubt,

to do it always with trust, method, or purpose.

"Victoria and Erasmus, when you apply trust and good faith to doubt, you neutralize it. When you apply method by sticking to discipline and verification of facts to doubt, you overwhelm it. When you confront doubt with your purpose and goals, you crush it," states a spirited Felicia Pointdexter.

The fortunate encounter marks the beginning of a life-long relationship between Erasmus and Mrs. Pointdexter. In the years to come, all the way up to her retirement, she will end up spending countless hours providing invaluable tutelage to him.

Royal Cambridge Scholastic Institute (2019)
(University's Auditorium)

Professor Cromwell-Smith returns to the present with a smile of remembrance for the erudite librarian.

"When in doubt, revert to its antidotes including the most potent of them all, purpose."

"Professor, why are doubts so pervasively nagging?" asks a tall, young red-haired girl with a southern accent.

"It is very easy to sit down and while commiserating, doubt everything and everyone, and do nothing. Doubts without its three antidotes are just fake walls built out of lame excuses. So always remember, when in doubt apply trust, method or purpose."

"See you all next week," states the eminent professor as the student body is left to realize and ponder that the August pedagogue may have just gifted them the formula of how to do away with doubts and vacillations.

Then, as he walks outside towards his old rusty bike, the inspired professor immediately takes in the magnificent spring day. Fittingly, he is in for a surprise. At first, he doesn't recognize his bike. It has a basket sitting atop the front wheel cover that is clipped to the handlebar. It's filled to capacity and has a red and white checkered mantle on top. He lifts it and sees a collection of pastries, cheeses, fruits, and a card. He opens it and as he reads it, his heart is inundated with joy and infatuation.

"It is true that trust, method, and purpose do away with doubt. But what really trumps it, getting rid of it for good, is true love." Instinctively, he lifts his head and there she is on her bike with her own picnic basket and five balloons.

"What are you waiting for?" she asks and in an instant pedals away. Erasmus mounts his bike and chases her. That's when he sees the writing on each globe.

On one globe, the second largest, it reads, "when in <u>doubt</u>, apply ..." "trust", "method", or "purpose". And on the biggest of them all with heart-shaped dimensions, his eyes widen in surprise and joy, as he looks at the huge letters - "And True Love Trumps Them All."

CHAPTER 15

DUALITY

Charles River, Boston (2019)

The nascent light of a new day filters its way throughout the river's magnificent nature. Sun rays painted with soft reddish and pale yellow colors, take their time illuminating the silent landscape. The remains of scattered fog patches, dissolve as they lazily rise up to the sky, giving way to a magnificent but extremely cold, spring day. Only the synchronized oar splashes can be heard, along with the heavy breathing of the twosome gasping for air, as they move at moderate speed along the quiet waters with a steady and rhythmic pace. Erasmus and Victoria have been rowing for the better part of a half an hour when they reach their destination.

In a familiar corner within the river banks, they tie up their rowing boat, and following a perfectly rehearsed routine, each extracts from their tiny backpacks tightly bundled matching bodysuit warmers and put them on.

Then, holding hands, the enamored pair strolls for a couple of hundred yards and heads to one of their favorite morning places in town, a tiny French Boulangerie with plenty of chairs and tables outside - a perfect spot to enjoy gallic treats in the outdoors, right by the river's edge.

"Dear, I would like to visit your hometown, someday," she pleads as they wait to be served their usual basket of French bread and pastries along with their café au laits.

"My lady, nothing will give me greater pleasure," he says mulling it over. His eyes are suddenly wide open in realization, and with a big tender smile he continues.

"Tell you what, we'll go over there this summer, then we can travel by train throughout the old continent. I've always dreamed about traveling with you across Europe," he says staring intensely at her, while softly caressing her hand with the tips of his fingers.

"I've only been there a few times, mainly for conferences, so you'll have to show me everything and take me everywhere, but with lots of patience," she pleads bundled up in emotions and excitement.

"It'll be my pleasure my lady," he responds, willing to oblige his love of her traveling dreams and desires.

A distant thunder is an ominous signal of a possible change in the idyllic weather. Instantly, Erasmus sees the change of expression as clouded emotions quickly get the best of Victoria. Through her eyes, Erasmus sees Vicky traverse across her whole emotional spectrum. At first, her eyes are nervous as anger flashes through, but thankfully it leaves in no time; then, seemingly her orbits are bouncing all over as if wanting to leave in a hurry; then, obfuscation takes over again, until finally her gaze focuses back on Erasmus. Realizing she has been made, her blue irises denote surprise. So, softness erupts and a sparkle suddenly appears, followed by an affirmative twinkle. Finally, relief becomes evident and happiness prevails. With her eyes shining, Victoria finally smiles as his hand, ever so slightly, tightens the grip a bit more, reassuring her as he has always done.

"There was a time when I could not control my fears about thunder," she says.

"With good reason my lady, if lightning struck so close to you as a child, it is quite understandable that subsequently, you developed this phobia," he says, just tagging along with her thoughts.

Victoria gazes at Erasmus for a long time, as if trying to decide how to react. Then, all of a sudden, it all comes out, as it always does, in the form of an eruption.

"You are so utterly inept at faking anything, my adorable Brit," she suddenly says bursting in laughter.

"My lady, why would I disrupt your beloved fantasy about your childhood mishap?" he defends himself.

"Because you know that I don't really mean to talk about it," she says lightheartedly.

"You mean that your problem with bad weather is that in the past it was a telltale need for perfection in your life. Always, there seemed to be something wrong or incomplete in the best of moments and circumstances, even if they were extraordinary or magnificent," he says, now being blunt, once she opened the door for him.

"Yes, it was like that, if it wasn't perfect the day was ruined, and that took away so many moments I could've enjoyed immensely if I would've taken the bad with the good," she reasons aloud in a spontaneous monologue.

"But my lady, look at you nowadays. It's a remarkable change for the better. Your natural instincts are still the same, but you're able to rationalize them and see through the banality of it all, before reacting negatively or blocking yourself out," Erasmus says, reassuring her with proud eyes.

"Having you next to me makes it a lot easier, dear," she offers in gratitude to Erasmus.

"Do you remember how we found the solution to such affliction?" Victoria suddenly asks.

"How could I forget? Mrs. Pointdexter, good old Mrs. Pointdexter, doted us with a timeless treasure, about the perils of contemplating the world through extremes," he replies remembering promptly the unforgettable session.

"That was a memorable day at the Harvard library. Mrs. Pointdexter's lesson about duality was timeless," she says, remembering vividly with big wide eyes.

Then, as it happens with tightly knit couples, it hits them both at the same time. They look at each other in realization and then smile knowing exactly what the other is thinking.

"Fittingly, I'll make duality the subject of today's class," he says with pensive eyes as they finish their breakfast. An hour later as Victoria drives Erasmus to class, they remember the diminutive and stern librarian that patiently sat with them on countless occasions throughout the years.

Royal Cambridge Scholastic Institute (2019)
(University's Auditorium)

As they approach the university buildings, Vicky performs her usual magic on him.

"Dear, today you're in possession of a precious gift for your students. Go and be the best you can be, so they can be doted with all of its priceless dimensions." Thus, along with a warm and cozy kiss, her words fire him up into an inspired state. So he marches with poetic strides and careless whistling to class in a state of total bliss as if walking over clouds.

"How's everyone today?" asks a spirited professor.

"Insanely awesome, professor," replies an enthusiastic student body.

"Class, sometimes in life we tend to view people, the world and life itself, as choices between opposites. We cannot see but two options and we obsess about taking one or the other. Thus, we become trapped in an existence, where we contemplate everything as a duality, where we always push ourselves into a corner and see no other alternative but to pick between what we believe are the only alternatives available to us."

The professor continues to everyone's undivided attention.

"Duality is an issue that haunted both Victoria and I throughout our childhood and teen years, until an endearing librarian mentor provided us with a timeless life lesson, one that forty years later, is still at work for both of us," explains the professor. "Let me take you back in time. The story begins like this ..."

Erasmus and Victoria's Studio,
Boston (1977)

In the early morning hours, young Erasmus goes out for a run while his other half stays sleeping for a bit longer. When Vicky wakes up, her first sight is one of a glass of fresh orange juice lying right in front of her on the bedside table. Immediately after, she sees the flower arrangement with a card and her heart stops. The red roses are sparkling and fully bloomed. The card reads, "May life continue to give us the magic of true love forever. My beloved lady, you are cordially invited to an afternoon in the park with me. It'll be a picnic for two. I'll fetch you up at exactly twelve 0'clock at the library." She chuckles and rejoices, inundated with the enchantment of her Brit wizard. Seemingly, it all bodes well for a magnificent day. But her premonition proves to be not long-lived, as shortly after she promptly erases all of her feel-good spirit, with her obsession for perfection, making happiness or love, virtually impossible.

Predictably, the morning does not go well for Victoria Emerson-Lloyd. The moment she steps out the door, her day takes a turn for the worst, as an uncomfortable light rain and fog is present. Then, the occasional thunder roars, far away in the distance, unsettling her even more.

'Why on this particular day does bad weather show up and ruin the picnic Erasmus prepared for the two of us,' she reasons totally obfuscated.

Harvard's Widener Library (1977)

Arriving at the magnificent library before noon, with time to spare, Victoria sits with her former roommate Gina, fuming. Vicky totally forgets to greet her mentor, good old Mrs. Pointdexter.

'What is it with young Victoria? Each time she is upset about something her good manners go out the window,' observes the wise librarian as unintendedly she listens to each one of Vicky's inappropriately loud remarks.

Oblivious to her surroundings, Victoria proceeds to describe her morning in great detail to her best friend - how well everything started and how it was suddenly spoiled. Gina is restless and wants to talk about something else, but Victoria goes on and on, not realizing that sensing her growing ambivalence about her future with Erasmus, Gina is determined to bring clarity into what she believes is a needless and reckless attitude from Vicky.

"Victoria, why would you try to force Erasmus to move to your hometown if he wants to marry you, why spoil true love?" asks Gina incredulously.

"Because that's the only way it'll work out between us," Victoria answers adamantly.

"You've not yet given me a valid reason to justify a forced move," refutes Gina.

Victoria stays silent without answering. She is boiling and frustrated inside. But Gina isn't prepared to let it go yet.

"And the reason you haven't is because you don't have a single real reason. The fact is that it's not convenient to go back home even for you. Your future is here," adds Gina.

"But my family is all over there," Vicky argues half-heartedly.

"You moved over here running away from your family and your hometown. Who are you kidding? Yourself?" snaps back Gina.

Victoria's eyes are darting in every direction and seemingly lost.

"Vicky, guilt-driven-love does not work; to expect this particular Brit to do what you want, out of making him feel guilty if he doesn't bend to your wishes, is a recipe for disaster with him. I'm telling you, it won't work. Neither will, transactional-driven love, like if you come, we'll marry, if you don't, we won't. No can do, Vicky. Tid for tad will fail with him as well. But, what you're going to do for sure, is to spoil what you've got," Gina states matter of factly.

'Maybe Gina is right, he'll never do it,' Vicky thinks with premonition and realization.

As the wall clock marks twelve o'clock, Victoria's sunny Brit shows up and walks briskly towards the two friends.

"Ladies, it's a pleasure to see you both." Bowing his head slightly, he announces in words from another place, even another era, and as usual, totally oblivious to what has just taken place.

Erasmus immediately notices that Gina and Victoria are displaying cursory smiles. "What's going on here?" he asks in surprise.

"I'll tell you young man, I'll describe to you what's really going on, better than your utterly spoiled girl," interjects uninvitedly, Mrs. Pointdexter, the stern and strict head of their University's library.

Gina, Victoria, and Erasmus turn in her direction with incredulity and total surprise.

"Mrs. Pointdexter, how are you?" states Erasmus with a big smile as he extends his hand to greet her.

"Not so well, as I've been listening to the most banal and superficial conversation I've heard in years," she replies admonishing the startled Victoria right off the bat.

"But that was a private conversation," Gina blurts, fighting back trying to defend her friend, but Pointdexter cuts her off.

"No, it wasn't private, not only were you breaking the rules of the library, and perhaps should have been thrown out of the building, you were talking so loud that lots of people in this place, not only me, overheard everything that you said," Mrs. Pointdexter states with severity.

Both girlfriends sit quietly with contrite and embarrassed faces. Erasmus then winks at Mrs. Pointdexter, indicating his consent to go on.

"As I'm sure this is a pattern that repeats itself often, with your permission, I would like to read for you all, a perfect antidote to what is afflicting our immature young lady today," she adds seeking approval.

"It'll be an honor Mrs. Pointdexter, please go ahead and get the scribble," Erasmus states while both girls provide their consent, by sheepishly nodding their heads.

The diminutive lady then disappears with quick steps that are bursting with determination. They can see her in the distance as she climbs a short ladder, then, in exacting movements, she retrieves a book that's thin in pages but huge in dimension. In no time she comes back, sits right in front of them and starts to read …

Duality

Here is the problem with Duality.

At first sight, it seems to be something it isn't,

like a state of deliberate indecisiveness

or even ignorant and willful duplicity,

between choices.

Duality is quite the contrary to what it appears to be,

at least as far as this verse goes ...

We stumble into duality in life when,

either we crave, not one,

but the totality of choices ahead of us,

or we see everything and everyone

as a two-sided proposition of

"either or."

Not enough has been said about

the first kind of duality,

consisting of the capricious art of wanting it

both ways in life,

of wanting it all, simultaneously and at any cost,

no matter what,

where, who, when, why, or how.

This usually leaves no room for anything

or anyone else.

This voraciousness, in most cases

is in itself a problem,

not only because we seldom enjoy either one,

but also, because in addition,

malignant-greedy-duality is nothing

but a pernicious existential

waste of time,

a pointless and fruitless exercise

in instant and constant gratification,

which is not only banal and empty,

but above all, devoid of any meaning and purpose, hence not

transcendental,

meaning that we are not "living" nor "alive"

when we practice it

or chase it.

On the other hand,

when duality is polarizing,

we see the universe, the world, life, and its people,

through opposing extremes,

antagonizing sides

and irreconcilable differences, all of the time.

Everything around us becomes,

black or white, good or evil, exhilarating or angsty, fulfilling or

empty, happy or depressive,

crowded or lonely,

entertaining or boring, truthful or false,

faithful or treasonous,

and real or fake.

Everyone we interact with becomes,

either superior or lesser, affluent or deprived,

healthy or unwell, successful or a failure,

entitled or a parasite,

solvent or a social ballast,

with us or against us,

able or handicapped,

free or condemned,

innocent or scarlet letter bearers,

socially adequate or psychopaths.

Our emotional and rational lives are either,

controlled or chaotic, effusive

or filled with resentment, exuberant

or frustrated, on a high or on a low,

abstinent or viced,

carnivorous or vegan, nice or nasty,

generous or greedy and selfish.

But, the shining light and lasting beauty of life,

lies not on opposite sides, but right down the middle.

A wholesome life is driven by virtues,

that reside strictly and solely between extremes.

They are located in the area of confluence

where we ponder and tinker

with all of our existential levers.

Then, instead of a world of pairs or duos,

of either "a" or "b" choices,

we find a third alternative,

made out entirely from both extremes.

That's where and how life

can be brought into balance,

and why, it is only in the middle where most,

if not all our existential virtues can be found,

namely temperance, uniqueness, out

of the norm prudence, good judgment,

patience, endurance, tolerance,

forgiveness, a good heart, creativity,

artistry, open-mindedness,

clarity, cautiousness,

meditative and contemplative states,

repentance, generosity, gratitude,

moderation, hope, inspiration,

frugality, faith, change, evolution,

our conscience, our spirit, and our soul.

Duality by nature is incomplete and unfulfilling,

as it deprives us

of all of the available choices,

sending us into extremes, as well

as absolute and rigid positions.

Duality can be dangerous

as it casts opposite or extreme sides

against each other,

creating potential or real conflicts and clashes

between the parties, based on the simple and

diminimous desire, of one side prevailing over the other at any

and all costs.

Duality also casts blindness

in our hearts, spirits, and souls,

depriving us of the ability

to experience life and enjoy the

universe, the world, nature,

and others simply because we ignore the third choice,

that of contemplating life halfway through extremes,

right down the middle.

As Mrs. Pointdexter finishes the scribble, Erasmus, Victoria, and Gina are left staring at her with luminous eyes as if a gigantic dark veil has been lifted off of them.

"Thank you, Mrs. Pointdexter," Victoria babbles sheepishly, as the two others instinctively let her take the lead.

"Victoria, you wake up and receive this wonderful gesture from your infatuated Brit – beautiful flowers, a card, a freshly squeezed juice, and an invitation for a romantic picnic just for the two of you. I wish I had someone to do those wonderful things for me. And yet, you manage to get yourself obfuscated about the weather. What's wrong with you? Life is too short my dear. Take all the good and block out the bad stuff. Rarely if ever is life perfect, convenient or not trying," Mrs. Pointdexter says in conclusion.

"This is a lesson, I will never forget Mrs. Pointdexter. This is the first time I see it crystal clear, and I promise you that from now on, I'll do the utmost to get a grip on myself, in order to stay out of my own way, so I can enjoy the best life has to offer, no matter how flawed or incomplete it may be," states Victoria in gratitude.

Mrs. Pointdexter hurries back to her duties with a look of certitude and satisfaction that her message was received by all three youngsters. Shortly after, Victoria, Gina, and Erasmus walk out of the library arm in arm, as if possessed by a powerful and brand new existential tool.

Royal Cambridge Scholastic Institute (2019)
(University's Auditorium)

"Class, as you reflect back on the subject of duality and its perils; focus on the only place where virtue can be found in life – the middle ground not the extremes," the professor states in conclusion.

"Professor, in our previous class we covered the subject of doubt. How are duality and doubt related?" asks a long-haired young man.

"That's an excellent question. They are actually closely linked. Doubt surges out of our inability to decide between extremes or absolutes and our incapacity to see the middle ground and thus, escape duality," clarifies the professor, to the realization of the entire student body, as can be judged by their nodding faces.

"Professor Cromwell, doesn't society have to evolve first before many more of us as individuals can seek and embrace the middle ground?" asks a young Chinese female student.

"Wonderful question. Our civilization certainly has to reach a different and higher level in our social behavior and belief system in order to evolve out of the duality-driven environment that we are currently in. This type of evolution is not only needed but is our next level up; and it is being pointed to us, even from the world of science. For example, the next frontier in information technology is Quantum computing. At present and not coincidentally, same as with real life, the computer world is all based on the binary system of 1's and 0's. Quantum computing is based on a third state, a kind of trinary system (qubits) that involves both choices 1 and 0 at the same time, multiplying exponentially the processing power of a computer."

Professor Cromwell-Smith stares at his class for what seems an eternity. Without exception, the participants are all looking at themselves under the prism of duality, hopefully realizing the perils and narrowness of living under its shackles.

CHAPTER 16

GENIALITY

Royal Cambridge Scholastic Institute (2019)
(Erasmus and Victoria's Campus Home)

"Here we are forty years later and in many ways, nothing has changed in us as a couple. We love each other as we did then. But as individuals we have changed. My doubts have now become guilt and yours have morphed into fear. We've also had quite different life experiences," states a pensive Victoria, as they lay in bed at dawn.

As today is the last class of the academic year, Erasmus' mind is somewhere else.

"Dear, where in the universe are you?" she asks.

Erasmus gazes at her with deep eyes and a wide smile.

"My lady, love isn't perfect. There are always things missing, not working or not attainable, but we focus on and enjoy those, that we do have," states Erasmus turning philosophical.

'That's it! He just stopped me right in my tracks and again he wasn't even paying attention,' she reasons, feeling caught at the beginning of an act.

But on this morning, for some reason, she just wants to poke holes in their idyllic perfection.

"How is it that you lived a monastic life for forty years?" she suddenly asks with a skeptical tone.

"Where are you going with this?" he asks uneasily.

"I just want to know," she says capriciously.

"Why?" he asks defensively.

"Perhaps because it is so hard to comprehend," she says, sounding hollow but trying to justify herself.

"That's it, lack of understanding?" he asks not completely convinced.

"A bit of jealousy as well," she finally acknowledges.

"Now, we are talking," he says, lauding the truth.

"That's what you wanted right? To hear that I am jealous," she says acting hurt.

"Not really," he replies dismissively.

"Of course not, big Erasmus, sitting high up on Mount Olympus does not believe or feel it. How do you define jealousy? Yes, I remember now – those are just games people play," she says chastising him.

"Ok Victoria, I realize that this big scene has a reason. What do you want to know?" he asks trying to nail the subject.

"No girls, for forty years?" she asks with the expression of a teenager playing with fire.

"I never said that I was monogamous. No true love for four decades is what I said," he clarifies.

"Oh, so there were girls," she shoots back in surprise now with her hand scalded by the fire.

"A few," he replies cryptically.

"How many?" she presses with a knot in her throat.

"I did not keep count," he answers trying to avoid the subject.

"What two, three, ten, twenty?" she insists.

"Victoria look at you, what are you doing? A futile and masochistic exercise of chasing water under the bridge," he states trying to dodge the subject.

"Never close to something serious?" she persists relentlessly.

"Once," he replies.

"Who?" she asks still hunting for the truth.

"My first book editor," he answers matter of factly.

"What happened?" she asks needing to know more.

"I realized, it was only success-driven-love," he answers.

"Translate, please," she pleads in ignorance.

"This particular editor paid no attention to me when I was starting out as a writer, but afterwards she was infatuated with my success more than with me. Without it, she wouldn't have been there and I concluded there was no future with her," he reveals.

"Isn't that normal behavior?" she asks. Then, she immediately realizes that she has just made a crucial mistake with him.

"Not for me, Victoria," he answers, without an iota of amusement in his voice.

Silence finally dawns on them as if the eruption has run its course. But she knows better. 'He is not done,' she reasons accurately.

"My lady, you just blurted out the other reason why you left. Success or lack of thereof … fears …," he says in realization.

Victoria's eyes cloud up in an instant and she feels unmistakably guilty.

"This is simply your way of getting it out in the open," he says. He holds both her hands with a soft grip, and kissing them alternatively, finishes.

"She was eight years my junior and very attractive. I remember that after dating her for more than three years, I still had reservations about her. Then, one good night, she asked if I was ever going to pop the question," he narrates.

"Did you?" she asks.

"I remember that I replied with a question," affirms Erasmus.

Victoria listens on pins and needles.

"Would you have been interested in me if you didn't know about my success? And she was bluntly honest. No, she said, and that was the end of it," he explains.

"Ironically, on the issue of parity between a couple, to me the only way that the matter of success is overcome by love, is when success isn't known or hasn't yet arrived, or it starts right at the onset of the relationship, he continues.

"So, the fact that when we got back together, I didn't know you had become so successful as a writer, was huge for you," she affirms in expectation.

"You have no idea how huge Victoria," he sternly confirms.

She feels relieved, but at the same time foolish. She completely forgot the fabric her Brit is made of.

'I don't even remember how that fabric is cut and tailored either,' she reasons, scolding herself, while realizing the need to reacquaint herself with it, quickly. The sooner, the better.

"Dear, you know about the adjustments I made when we reunited. But, what did you do yourself?" asks Vicky finally turning the tables.

Erasmus stares at her with the kind of utter calmness she has always loved about him as it makes her feel safe and protected.

"My lady, what has driven our love isn't guilt, wealth, or lack thereof. What you have done since we were reunited, has been driven not so much by words, but strictly by facts and feelings," he says with profound accuracy.

"Facts?" she asks, not getting it.

"What I mean by facts are actions expressed in the form of boundless small gestures and teeny-tiny details we've shared with each other from the beginning," he replies with eyes of plentitude.

"My fearless, unmaterialistic, Brit," she declares hugging him with pride.

"Dear, what's the subject of your class going to be today?" she quizzes.

"Geniality," he replies with a rattled tone of voice.

The single word drops like a heavy weight right between them. Her face is now pained, but her eyes reflect understanding.

"Is this your last class of the year?" she asks rhetorically.

"Yes," he replies.

"I see," she says absentmindedly.

"No worries my lady, I am ready for it," he reassures her.

"In that case, go and kill that tiger, dear. I am sure you'll do a masterful job," she says gathering as much strength as her anguished self allows her.

A bit later, as Professor Cromwell-Smith leaves on his old rusty bike, Victoria watches him pedal away through the window – she cries a little. She knows that in a short while, he'll be talking about the day she vanished. At least it gives her comfort that earlier in the week she was able to "fill in" the blanks for him on what she had done exactly on her runaway day.

Professor Cromwell-Smith's bike sways with the vagaries of his own thought process. Today, his path is pointing to the future, but his wake is filled with nostalgia.

'She is right. We are both scarred survivors of a long and winding road. But you know what? We made it and here we are with plenty of life ahead of us,' he reasons.

Royal Cambridge Scholastic Institute (2019)
(University's Auditorium)

"How's everyone today?" the spirited professor asks.

"Awesome!" is the collective response.

"Hmm," he blurts, not quite satisfied with his right hand on his chin.

"OK, let's do that again," he urges them.

"How's everyone today?" the professor tries again.

"Insanely awesome!" the student body responds in unison.

"Right on," he says, now satisfied.

With the auditorium's energy still in crescendo, he commences their academic year's last journey.

"Today, we conclude our course with the subject of genius and geniality. In this, our last class, I'll be taking you to a remarkable day where two contrasting sides of life presented themselves – one like a comet that came and left in an instant, and the other as a discovery of one of those types of treasures that you hold onto for the rest of your life."

"It begins like this ..."

Harvard (1977)
(Erasmus and Victoria's Studio)

Victoria has been staring at the letter she's not supposed to read for a long time ...

In part, the letter states, "Mrs. V before I leave you, there is something else. Are you ready? ... I want to propose. Yes! I do, I want with all my heart for Victoria to be my wife and companion forever."

Vicky's reaction is utter fear. She wants to run and bolt out of the situation. For hours, Victoria sits totally paralyzed as she loses touch with time. When she finally sees the hour, all hell breaks loose.

She has to hurry up. Erasmus will be waiting for her at the train station in one hour for their trip to Cape Cod. But she's having a panic attack.

'Isn't this what you wanted since the day you met him?' she asks herself with no answer.

'A professor, that's all he'll ever be,' she quibbles against her crying heart, with the same obsessive and lame excuse.

'He's way too smart for me as well,' she reasons as the hole in her heart continues to grow and seemingly knows better than her where she's heading - which is literally going off a cliff. The phone rings which snaps her out of her dark cloud, but just for a moment.

"Hi mom," she says with a trembling greeting while picking up the wall-mounted handset.

"Sweet daughter of mine, have you made up your mind?" her mom asks while delicately putting pressure on her.

And, at that precise moment, Victoria finally succumbs to the self-inflicted pressure and excuses. She simply loses it! She goes off the rails not only altering the course of her life but also putting herself on a path of self-destruction.

"Yes," Victoria replies.

"And?" her mom quizzes in suspense.

"I just said it, yes," she fatefully says not really knowing what she is doing.

"How wonderful. You have no idea how happy this makes all of us. I'll go and tell everyone right away. When are you coming?" asks her mom joyfully and in total relief.

"Today," Victoria replies seemingly setting fate upon herself.

"But, don't you have classes?" her mom asks without really meaning it.

"I'm quitting mom, I want to get it done and start a family," replies another Victoria, the rational one, surfacing from entombment and taking over the enamored side of her. Her mother doesn't argue with it as this is what she has been advocating all along. She's simply in ecstasy as all she's ever known and what she was raised to be, is a housewife, which is exactly what she wants for her daughter.

"I'm sure that you know very well what you're doing Victoria. We'll welcome you back with open arms dear. Can't wait to see you. I'll go now and tell everyone. Bye," her mother says as she hurries to end the call to go and announce the "good news" to everyone.

Boston Main Train Station (1977)

With all her things packed in two suitcases, Victoria walks through Boston's train station feeling miserable.

'You are betraying his and your own heart,' she reasons as she cries a torrent of teardrops. When she enters the main hall, she still has a choice. She can choose to walk towards him and board the train to the Cape or she can walk to the Chicago-bound train and lose the love of her life – seemingly forever.

'Where is she?' thinks a nervous Erasmus as there are less than ten minutes till departure. He wants to go and look for her in the main hall, but he's afraid that he'll miss her at the agreed spot.

She stops and prays for divine guidance. 'If he finds me here, I won't be able to go home,' she cautions, as part of her wants to be spotted.

Five minutes are left until the train to the Cape departs. What to do? He can't miss the conference. He decides to go and check the main hall.

Victoria walks reluctantly and slowly towards the Chicago-bound train and as she leaves the main hall, her heart jumps at the sight of him in the distance. She stops. Dejection. It's not him. She continues to walk, now with her head down, and moving inexorably towards her prescribed and heartless future.

'Is that her?' he thinks for a moment. But the lady with two suitcases and her head down is heading in the opposite direction and is quickly swallowed up by the crowd.

'She is not here!' he panics as he pans the busy hall. Feeling dejected, Erasmus heads back and boards his train. 'Surely something came up. She'll be on a later train. I just hope that nothing happened and she's safe,' he reasons trying to justify her absence.

The date is December 15, 1977, twenty-two months after they first met. It's a day neither of them will ever forget.

Cape Cod (1977)

"Where's your other half?" asks his host and mentor, Scottish antiquarian Colin Carnegie, as he welcomes Erasmus at the hotel's front door.

"I don't know, she didn't make it to the train station on time. But I'm hoping she'll catch the next train," replies Erasmus.

"Did you have a fight or something?" asks Carnegie.

"Not at all," responds Erasmus.

"Do you want to use the phone and check on her?" his old trusted Scottish mentor asks.

"Perhaps I should, yes," says an anxious Erasmus. He calls home first, but there's no answer. Then he calls Victoria's best friend and former roommate. It takes a while for the Harvard switchboard to get a hold of Gina.

"Erasmus, what's up? Has something happened?" asks a surprised Gina, sensing it must be really important for him to be calling her.

"Vicky didn't show up at the station. We were planning on spending the weekend at Cape Cod at an antiquarian's conference. Could you check at the apartment for me please and make sure she's OK," he pleads.

"Of course, I have a key. Call me back in an hour," Gina replies already having a very bad gut feeling about it.

"I will. Thanks Gina," Erasmus says in confirmation.

"Anytime," Gina replies before hanging up with a tone not only of worry but of premonition as well.

"Erasmus, I don't want to impose on you but what I've organized can't wait. We can cancel it if you want. It's up to you," Carnegie offers.

Erasmus sits still for a while. 'I can't just disregard Mr. C's kind gesture of bringing us all the way down here. I'm sure she'll eventually turn up,' Erasmus reasons.

"Not at all Mr. C, let's do it," he answers in earnest.

With a broad smile, the Scottish antiquarian leads Erasmus through the hotel lobby into an adjacent small conference room.

"Every two years we have this weekend retreat for all the New England antiquarians and librarians," Mr. C informs him.

"We were so excited when we got your invitation," replies Erasmus in gratitude.

"You'll get to know all of the antiquarians as they gather after the sessions. They all know about you two already," Carnegie adds.

Erasmus is not surprised as he has come to understand just how tightly knit the old book antiquarian community is.

'What matters now, is to show gratitude for how well they've treated us,' he mulls over. 'Whatever they have in store, you must accept it graciously and with open arms,' he reminds himself.

"Mr. C, what is it about tonight that is so pressing?" asks an intrigued Erasmus.

"Well, it's a surprise - you'll find out soon enough," Mr. C replies.

The Cape Cod Unexpected Bend in the Road

They walk into the room and Erasmus is immediately taken aback in shock and wonder as the five occupants sitting at the round table all stand up with warm and welcoming smiles. There they are, Mrs. Peabody, Mrs. Pointdexter, Mr. Faith, Mr. Lafayette, Mr. Ringwald, and with Mr. Carnegie that makes six. Erasmus immediately recognizes that there are eight chairs at the table.

"She couldn't make it on time to the station, you'll meet her tomorrow," he preempts them.

Erasmus shakes hands with each one of his mentors, kissing the two ladies on both cheeks, the European way. Then, he takes a seat where indicated.

"Young Erasmus, we've all discussed in advance what to do on this rare occasion of all of us having the opportunity to meet and sit with you. It is a real pity that Victoria is not here. But,

I'm sure that you'll convey to her what we review here with you today," Mr. Carnegie solemnly states.

Erasmus nods unconvincingly at the suggestion.

"Young man, we want to talk to you about one subject that we all agree holds the key to your future," states Mrs. Peabody.

"Let us all first share a number of anecdotical lessons with you, as they will lead us into the subject matter," states Mr. Lafayette.

"I'll start first if you all allow me," Mr. L states. Everyone in the room consents.

"Erasmus, the first anecdote is about illusions in life," announces Mr. Lafayette.

The Case of the Magnificent Illusionist
(Mr. Lafayette)

"In my last year in high school, I was part of a soccer team that won the state championship for the third year in a row. Just before graduation, my parents asked how I wanted to vacation before starting college. My answer was that I would love to go to Europe to watch my favorite pro soccer teams. Thus, as a graduation present, they sent me across the Atlantic with three of my closest teammates. During the summer we traveled by train and cheered with the hooligans at Chelsea playing Manchester at Wembley, then we saw Bayern play Borussia at Munich, Saint Germain play Marseille at Paris and Real Madrid play Barca at Barcelona. On our last weekend, we arrived in Italy to watch A.C. Milan play at home against Rome. We decided to spend Friday night in nearby Florence and then spend Saturday, the day before the match, wandering around the magnificent city. It all started the next day when we were admiring Michelangelo's David at the galleria. A young kid ran by handing out fliers. He gave me one and it immediately caught my attention as it was written both in Italian and English. "Come and experience the greatest illusionist on earth, don't miss it, Teatro di la buonna fortuna, 8:00 p.m." After reading it, I persuaded the others to go to the show with me. At the theatre, we were in for a treat. The illusionist's specialty was to disappear. One moment he would be on center stage and in a split second he would vanish. He would reappear in the back row of the hall. He did this with his assistant as well, but only after he cut her in half. Then, he did it with members of the audience and from their seats, poof! They vanished and "voila" reappeared on the balcony rows of the theater. But the grand finale defied the laws of gravity, logic, and common sense. An enormous elephant disappeared right in front of all of us.

'Genius.' I was in shock and awe about what we had just witnessed. Little did I know that the next day, I was going to be handed one of the greatest life lessons I've ever received.

"The day of the big game started inconspicuously enough with tens of thousands of 'tifosi' and us cheering before the clash got underway. And who suddenly appeared in the center of the field? None other than the illusionist. The announcer explained that on behalf of the homeless, something he once was himself, the illusionist would kick a penalty shot and try to beat Milan's goalie. The homeless charity would receive a hefty amount from the illusionist if he were to miss it. But, the donation would double if he made the goal. The entire stadium cheered for the popular artist. My first observation was that he was ill-fitted with the wrong shoes and oversized shorts. Then, as he started to dribble the ball, he looked rather clumsy. By the time he started running towards the ball to kick the penalty shot, I already knew the outcome. But, I wasn't prepared at all for what actually happened. Just before reaching the ball, the illusionist planted his left foot while his shooting leg loaded to the back. Then . . . debacle. His loose soccer boot literally hit the ground first and got buried in the turf. He tripped at sprinting speed, his body lurched forward in the air and he landed face-first at the startled goalie's feet. Needless to say, the illusionist suffered national embarrassment as it was covered by the Italian tabloid press ad nauseam. His popularity then took a nosedive and his amazing act shut down a few weeks later."

Erasmus is mesmerized and lost in the imagery just displayed to him.

"I'm sure that you're asking yourself what this anecdote has to do with Genius. Please bear with us as you will see, it goes to the heart of the matter," explains Mr. Lafayette.

"Mrs. Peabody the floor is all yours," states Mr. Lafayette yielding the floor.

The Case of the Wise and Benevolent Attorney
(Mrs. Peabody)

"Thank you, Lafayette. Erasmus, I'll be talking about the hardships of others. In my younger years after I graduated from law school, I clerked for a famous criminal attorney. During an ice storm, one of the partners of the law firm had a terrible automobile accident when a trailer truck lost its brakes and crashed into his car. He broke his back and was paralyzed from the neck down. Day after day, I accompanied my boss to visit his friend. The amazing thing about these visits was that, besides the pleasantries, they were normal work encounters where they went over every relevant case they were handling. Increasingly, my boss would tell me that his handicapped partner and he were now focusing much better on the cases, and the incremental productivity was paying benefits to them in regard to their law practice. Then, by year's end an ugly situation occurred. The other partners of the firm, who had rarely visited him, attempted to deny the handicapped partner's share of that year's profits by alleging that all he was doing, in his condition, was to serve as an assistant to my boss. My boss and the paralyzed attorney promptly quit the firm and went on to form one of the most successful law firms in New England. Shortly before I quit, in order to join the world of antique books, I was privileged enough to witness the two of them lawyering together - they were almost invincible. But it took one last case, for me to finally understand my boss' genius.

311

It happened like this. One of the most prominent businessmen in Boston was indicted on bribery of public officials, fraud, and money laundering. He also filed for bankruptcy and was unable to hire and pay for attorneys. So, it was a pro bono proposition. Nevertheless, many of the prominent attorneys in the city paraded through the prison where he was being held to offer their help to someone who had been a loyal friend through the years. However, he kept on rejecting one after another. The press and the public started to question his gratitude and the judge stated clearly that his patience was becoming exhausted - enter my boss. We visited the disgraced businessman several times over the course of a couple of weeks. On one of the occasions when we left from a visit, a reporter yelled a rhetorical question at us.

"You guys are the first that have lasted more than two visits. Did you know that?"

"No comment."

"A couple of days later we were retained. I wondered why he did it, as at no point in time, had the conversations been in regard to us being hired as his lawyers. Eventually, although I did not work for him any longer, my boss got him acquitted. Once out of prison, the man reinvented himself and became so successful that I have to assume that my former boss got paid in full. One thing I do know is that when my former boss ran unsuccessfully for Governor, the businessman financed his whole campaign," concludes Mrs. Peabody.

"Did you ever ask the businessman why he chose your boss?" asks Erasmus.

"Yes I did, but by that time I had already figured it out. We will cover that in detail at the end," wraps up Mrs. P with a broad and loving smile.

"Mr. Faith," states Mrs. P as she yields the floor to him.

The Case of the New York Cabbie
(Mr. Faith)

"Thank you. Dear Erasmus, my anecdote is about the average Joe, and it occurred while visiting New York City, inside of a yellow cab. At the time, I worked as an investment banker for one of the largest Wall Street firms and was stationed in London. I wasn't a happy camper as my limo hadn't shown up when I exited the arrivals terminal at JFK. After 15 minutes of waiting, I reluctantly boarded one of the dreaded banged up, smelly, bouncy, old New York taxi cabs. When right at the beginning, the driver made his first daredevil maneuver, I prayed we would make it into the city in one piece. How wrong I was about the driver because of my countless prejudices and stereotypes."

"Let me turn on the AC with a bit of a wild forest aroma," the driver stated with a heavy middle eastern accent. "I will also put the vehicle in limo driver mode and you'll not be bothered by the springy suspension when I drive steady," he said as was flashing a big smile.

"Thank you." I responded already somewhat relieved.

"You're American but you don't live here," the cabbie stated.

"How do you ...?" I started to ask, but he went on.

"And you haven't been here for a while. I picked it up by the way you look at everything," the driver observed with pinpoint accuracy.

"Are you always this observant?" I asked.

"It's my job," the driver replied.

"Aren't you just supposed to drive?" I asked teasing him. In reality, I was acting defensively as deep inside it rattled me a great deal that he was reading me so easily.

"Like, how do you call it, an automaton, a robot? So, I am not human to you?" the taxi driver responded with contempt, not liking my remark one bit. At that moment, I entered into a listening only mode as I was becoming curious.

"Or maybe dumb, right?" he asked with a voice now a tad too loud.

"Not at all sir, please go on. I want to listen to what you have to say," I offered opening the door for him to express himself freely.

"Well you will, like it or not, your type is always in need of regular guys like me, and a bit of common life roughing, to keep you in touch with reality," he said finally erupting like a menacing volcano.

Then, I just relaxed and let him go on.

"Over the course of driving a yellow cab in this city for over twenty-five years, babies have been delivered in my cab, lives of wounded or injured New Yorkers have been saved, life-saving medicines have been safely delivered, crimes have been stopped, marriages and couples have been engaged or broken and others have mended. People have been hired, others have been fired, dreams have started, and others have ended. I have prevented suicides and predicted others. I've had psychopaths, animals of prey, and molesters, I've had artists, directors, writers, politicians, and even former presidents in my yellow cab. I've delivered crucial documents. I've executed all the silliest chores that are an intrinsic part of the life of this city from carrying pampers to hand-delivering a note across town asking for forgiveness. I can read most men and many women. I can tell by people's accents where they come from. I see fakes, authentic and honest people as well as crooks. I've driven for hours from bar to bar for others to celebrate. I've had people and family getting back together after decades of being apart. I've translated for monks, mullahs, sheiks, imans, high clerics, rabbis, and priests. I've prayed with and for others. I've even given my car to a policeman chasing a bank robber - just like in the movies. I've also had thousands of kind and decent regular people that arrive in the city wearing eyes and faces filled with dreams, hope, and gratitude. Others that are just visiting have faces like those of children at an amusement park," concludes Mr. Faith.

Erasmus is absorbing and processing every single word. His senses are all in overdrive. With each piece of the story, his eyes widen more and more as if lights are turning on inside his head. "Mrs. Pointdexter, I yield to you," says Mr. Faith.

The Case of Order in Chaos in the Middle East
(Mrs. Pointdexter)

"Thank you, Mr. Faith," states Mrs. Pointdexter.

"Dear Erasmus, I'm going to narrate to you a life experience I had on the subject of chaos and other unsavory things in life. It took place in Dubai where I was attending a world conference of librarians. Several of my colleagues kept on suggesting that I go to the Old City Center where I would find all kinds of artifacts and ornaments typical of the Persian Gulf. They also recommended that I visit the shops selling precious metals, especially gold. Well, the ride over there was hectic to say the least. The driver claimed to have lost his way, so it took forever. Finally, we arrived. So, after paying what the meter showed, I stepped out of the car. Suddenly, I was in a steam bath as a wave of hot air hit me. Then, when I inhaled, the hot air burned through my entire respiratory system. Surrounding me were copious amounts of bubblicious, bearded men, in robes and sandals. I realized at that moment that I was utterly lost and I had no clue where I was. The place started to overwhelm me. So, instinctively I walked towards the water looking for a bit of sea breeze. Finally, I realized that I was in the middle of a port. Not one with gigantic boats, but quite the opposite, there were hundreds of small boats tied to one another. The activity was frantic. Goods, boxes, packages, and bags of all sizes were being loaded and unloaded in a totally chaotic fashion. All the men on the boats and around the dock were moving something or going somewhere. They looked scruffy with their beards and sunburned skins. For some reason that I did not understand at the time, the place caught my curiosity and I started to see what was really going on around me. After a while, I recognized the boats that were taking goods out, likely going to Iran I figured, then boats bringing in goods, probably Iranian products coming in for the local market. Of all the small merchant boats, I focused on one in particular. The tall man imparting orders was relentlessly directing others. It took me a while, but I figured out how he was organizing the goods by weight and type. I counted at least twenty different dispatchers delivering different types of products to his small vessel.

'Choreography in chaos,' I reasoned.

'That's powdered milk. Those are medicines,' I thought as I witnessed the pandemonium. Boat after boat kept leaving while others arrived. The action was filthy, noisy, chaotic, but far more efficient and effective than what I'd observed at first sight.

"Why doesn't Dubai service Iran with big-scale logistics?" Later on, I asked a U.A.E. officer at the conference.

His response was, "there's an international embargo on one side and on the other Iran has strict customs rules and taxes on imports," the officer replied.

'Brilliant, a constant drip of tailor-made shipments leaving every day to Iran and a channel for small Iranian exporters to send their goods and barter for sale here in Dubai,' I reasoned.

"In the end Erasmus, I learned in Dubai an important lesson directly relevant to the subject we are covering with you tonight," concludes Mrs. Pointdexter.

"Mr. Ringwald, the honor is all yours," Mrs. Pointdexter says yielding the floor.

The Case of the Big German Boss
(Mr. Ringwald)

"Thank you, Mrs. Pointdexter," states Mr. Ringwald a/k/a the Riddler.

"Dear young man, tonight I'll be speaking to you about knowing yourself. Years ago, before I entered the world of books, I worked for a multinational company that was based in Hamburg, Germany. The company was an American-owned, local enterprise. So, I was employed by the U.S. owners as an executive. However, the man in charge was a well-seasoned German man that had previously worked for almost thirty years for IBM Germany. In order to grow its market share, the company I was overseeing bought another enterprise in the south of Germany, in Munich. The German boss and myself, representing the American owners, went to Bavaria to welcome all the new employees to our organization. Everyone was assembled in one big auditorium where both he and I made brief statements followed by questions and answers. An employee stood up to ask a question to the big German boss from Hamburg. The live mic sat in the middle between the two of us. Seconds went by and the big boss did not answer. So, I turned to him to find out if there was anything wrong. But, he just sat there, clueless. Suddenly, forgetting about the mic that was live, he turned to me and asked in a whisper.

"Mr. Ringwald, did you understand the question?"

"Yes, of course. Do you want me to translate it for you?" I replied in jest.

"Yes please. No one can understand Bavarians in Germany but themselves," the big boss remarked forgetting about the mic. At that moment, the entire place burst into laughter.

"From then onwards, the joke of the evening became, Bavarian after Bavarian asking me to translate the questions for their big boss. But, one employee in particular, asked me a question that I've never forgotten and fittingly goes along with the overall story tonight. There was a young intern who stood up towards the end of the session and asked, "Sir, how do you compete?"

"You mean us as a corporation?" I replied.

"No, no you as an individual," the intern clarified.

"Well, let me think about it, as I've never been asked that before. How do I frame it?" I asked myself aloud.

"Alright, if you're competing against my strengths, my mindset is that I'm going to crush you. If you're competing against my weaknesses, I'm going to try to outwork and outlast you. If I still cannot beat you by then, I will join forces with you," I replied to the intern in the spur of the moment.

Later as we left, the big boss needed to dig deeper.

"Herr Ringwald, how come you understood that kid and I didn't?" the big boss asked me.

"When I first learned German, I didn't understand many of the phrases but understood some of the words. So, I learned how to get the overall meaning of the messages. Later on when I mastered the language, I still didn't forget that technique. In your case, if you don't understand one hundred percent of what is being said to you, you block it out and all of it becomes unintelligible," I replied.

"So, at the meeting, I walked out with two very important lessons that have served me well throughout my life and are both very relevant to tonight's subject," concluded Mr. Ringwald.

"Mr. Carnegie," says Ringwald yielding back to the Scottish antiquarian.

"Erasmus, now I'm going to read to you an early 20th century writing that will bring clarity to each and every story you've just heard.   After I'm through, we will all comment and draw conclusions and life lessons about the anecdotes."

Mr. Carnegie then begins to read in earnest ...

Geniality

If we are content

to oversimplify what Geniality is,

and limit ourselves

to mean it as something simply

cordial, affable, congenial,

gracious, sociable, cheerful, and kindly,

we rob the uniqueness and outstanding aspects of it.

Worst of all,

we trivialize the genius in all of us

which is an intrinsical part of our essence

and our sense of being.

Hence, the geniality we speak about in this scribble,

is only such that comes out of genius.

Here is the problem with genius,

we haven't figured it out yet,

what it means to be a genius?

What is to be genial, act genially, possess genialness and

geniality?

What is to be able to genialize ourselves, everyone, and

everything we touch?

The fact is, there is geniality inside each one of us,

it resides somewhere within

and it is ready and eager,

to be discovered, nurtured, developed, exploited,

and put into practice.

In a way, it's like our geniality is a genie in a bottle.

But, we make it really hard to become genial.

We think of genial in terms of

the most, exceptional, no one else,

and the absence of geniality as

less, common or everybody else.

We think of people and things in a binary way,

up or down.

Geniuses do neither of them.

In fact, quite the contrary,

genialness to begin with, levels the playing field.

Every day geniuses do not feel better

or less than others,

it is simply a term that does not exist

in their dictionary.

A genius is simply someone, anyone, everyone

that has recognized, discovered, or found

in himself or others,

the best talents and abilities he was born with,

and has uncorked, liberated,

and put them into practice.

Thus, a genius does not think

in terms of being better than others

or others being less than him.

He is simply really good at what he does best. Period.

Geniality can be found where we hold innate, unlimited,

and notable talent.

We are genial, any of us,

when we are able to tap into our

maximum potential and use our best strengths.

At such moments we get to use our superpowers

and become masters of our genius potential.

But don't ever confuse it with simplicity

as a genius only deals with hard stuff.

Nothing geniality tackles comes easy,

it is just that it looks

that way from the outside

in the hands of genial powers,

rehearsed talents, and innate abilities.

Ask yourself, what am I really, really good at?

What was I born and destined to be?

What is it that I am passionate about

and really love to do?

Honestly, what is it?

And given my abilities, passions, and talents,

what is it that I can do best in life?

And if I don't know it,

let me make it my life quest to find it.

One thing is certain, the genius in all of us

does not reside in those things

that we don't have the talent or the desire for.

The main obstacle and problem though,

is that geniality can be intimidating

and instead of embracing and getting close,

we shy away from it,

when in actuality what we need to do

is just the opposite.

In order to elevate ourselves,

we have to be surrounded by people

that have talents and abilities

that we aren't that good

or experienced at, or we simply don't have.

The absence of Geniality occurs

when we embark

on the futile and poisonous exercise

of comparing ourselves,

then envying the virtues and strengths of others,

often even worse,

when we do it against the backdrop

of our most notorious weaknesses and shortfalls.

Geniality is often confused

as being solely the spectrum

of those with extraordinary native intellectual power

or transcendental mental superiority,

inventiveness, and ability.

Geniuses are perceived

as profoundly gifted individuals

with attributes so diverse, complex,

and sophisticated

that we feel overwhelmed

and out of step in front of them.

The question we have to ask ourselves

in those cases is,

are we afraid?

Do we feel inadequate and intimidated

of extraordinary genius?

Or are we just afraid of ourselves?

Therefore, it is always healthy

to remind ourselves that,

Whatever someone else has,

we all have something else,

equally valuable in the universe of life.

It is also worth remembering that

we are all geniuses at one

or a few things where we shine and soar,

but we are all clumsy clowns

on many, many others.

Hence, the genius in us does not compare itself

To anyone or anything,

because it is not only pointless,

but a zero sum game

and our humbling flaws are always waiting for us,

on every other corner of the streets of life.

So, what are we waiting for?

Our genius eagerly awaits us.

Our genie in a bottle is ready

to be uncorked and liberated.

Let us unleash the genius inside all of us,

so we can perform at our maximum potential

and at the top of our abilities

and be the best we can be in life.

When Mr. Carnegie finishes the scribble, the mentors are ready for their closing arguments.

"Erasmus, I made a critical error of judgment looking down at the taxi driver that I met on that day. I soon found out that the man was genial at what he did. Was there any difference between him and myself, the investment banker? Absolutely not, we were at the same exact level, each one performing in life to the best of our abilities," states Mr. Faith.

"Young man, the genius and success behind my boss, the wise criminal attorney, was that he never looked down on people irrespective of their circumstances. For him, the fact that his partner was now a quadriplegic or his friend was in jail did not change one bit his perception of them and he continued to treat them exactly like before their mishaps. Hence, they reacted the same way towards him," explains Mrs. Peabody.

"Dear Erasmus, that day in Dubai I was faced with oppressive heat, chaos, filthiness, and noise in a foreign place and yet by not rejecting it, I found there was real geniality behind everything taking place. Always remember this, nothing genial comes easy as a genius always deals with hard and difficult things," states Mrs. Pointdexter.

"Dear young apprentice, that day in Germany, the big German boss did not tackle the obstacle of a different accent in his own country and opted for the easy way out. He thought of himself as better than his workers and blocked himself out. Then, when I replied to the young employee about competing with others, I was genial at accepting that in order to win, I had to be aware of my opponents as well as my strengths and weaknesses. I had to deploy my best abilities and efforts to win. There are no 'lone rangers' in the world Erasmus," remarks Mr. Ringwald.

"Young scholar, in Italy I engaged in the kind of behavior one has to avoid in order to be able to tap into geniality. When the illusionist performed, I thought he was pure and simply a genius. Then, when I saw him at the stadium, ill-dressed and clumsy with the ball, he was no longer a genius in my eyes. Then, when he tripped making his kick, I lost all my admiration for him. You see, we look at everything and everyone that way. Up or down. Geniality does neither," states Mr. Lafayette leaving the floor to Mr. Carnegie to sum it all up.

"Dear young fellow, at first Mr. Faith failed to recognize the genius in the taxi driver and almost missed a great opportunity to explore his world. It took Mrs. Peabody quite some time to recognize the genius in her criminal attorney boss, but in the end, she realized that he possessed the gift of recognizing and tapping the genius of others, regardless of their circumstances. In Dubai, Mrs. Pointdexter was curious enough to find geniusness in chaos. Also, Mr. Ringwald displayed geniality while understanding the local language better than a native and by demonstrating how to grow a business by tapping into his best talents and/or the talents of others. Finally, Mr. Lafayette showed us how the illusionist, in his eyes, was at first a genius but suddenly he wasn't when nothing had really changed - proving two key points. First, we look up and down at people and things when genialness does neither. And second, we all are genial at a few things but clumsy clowns at many others. Bottom line, all Mr. Lafayette saw at first when viewing the illusionist, was a human being in full display of his best talents and passions. He saw genius," states Mr. Carnegie summing it all up.

Erasmus can't contain his smile. His six hosts stand up and gather around him, and one by one hug and embrace him. He in turn obliges and kisses both ladies on both cheeks.

"Thank you," he says holding one hand on his heart.

"We're all certain that this encounter will help you achieve your maximum potential in life. Go and get some sleep and we'll see you tomorrow at the breakout sessions," states Mr. Carnegie in his parting words.

Erasmus walks out feeling that he has been graced with precious knowledge and wisdom that he'll treasure forever. Then, he turns his head one more time and waves at them in gratitude. "This was a magnificent gift," he says.

Erasmus heads back to his room in his typical absent-minded state, as he has gotten so engrossed in the mentor's session, that he has lost track of time and reality. He finally sees his watch and realizes that several hours have gone by since he spoke to Gina. Nerves quickly creep in, as it finally dawns on him that he forgot about Vicky. He rushes to the room and his heart sinks when he doesn't find her there. He then tries his home number but gets no answer. He immediately calls Gina, but it takes almost half an hour for Gina to make it to the college switchboard.

"Gina?" Erasmus asks.

"Erasmus, she did it," Gina replies in a matter of fact somber tone.

"She did what?" he asks in angst.

"She's gone Erasmus. She packed all her belongings and left town," Gina says delivering the devastating blow.

Royal Cambridge Scholastic Institute (2019)
(University's Auditorium)

Professor Cromwell-Smith is spent, but at the same time relieved. Just like the previous year, he has run out of words.

As he scans the audience, he sees Victoria and nods in gratitude. She stands up and starts to applaud with intensity and tears. He smiles reassured and proud that she is there and at last facing that painful and yet amazing day together with him. The entire auditorium now stands to cheer the exhausted erudite poet.

Once it subsides, he continues …

"You see, life sometimes presents us with pain or tragedy simultaneously with beauty, wonder, and renewal. That memorable day had both, a comet that came and left my universe in a hurry and simultaneously an amazing encounter with six caring, loving, and mentoring antiquarians that put forth their best efforts to give me the best possible wisdom anyone can receive," the professor concludes.

"Professor what about next year?" asks an eager student.

"We will have the same format, but next time we will revisit the long forty years Victoria and I lived apart."

Before he is ready to part ways, the erudite professor has one final thing to say.

"Always remember this – all of you have a genius inside. Your challenge is to recognize, learn and then use the best talents and abilities you were born with. Genius is to tap and deploy the best you've got inside - whatever that is. Your genie in the bottle is your genius. The genius in you is waiting. What are you waiting for?"

Erasmus again looks into the audience and sees Victoria with her hands over her heart as she says, "I love you," with her lips. He responds promptly and mimics her in the exact same fashion.

"That's all, see you next year," he says bowing his head. Then, as is his custom, he signals the movement of an orchestra conductor's hand and opens his arms. The entire audience in unison calls it like it is, "insanely awesome!"

Note by the Author,

When I was a toddler, tragically, my biological parents perished in a road accident. Erasmus and Victoria (who was my biological grandmother) adopted, raised, and provided me with a wonderful childhood and an extraordinary upbringing. But, just when I thought that Geniality was the final book; driven by an inexplicable curiosity and a gut feeling that there was more to be uncovered and understood about my parents' separation; for both reasons, even before "Geniality" was completed, I started working on a sequel. Then, as I dove into it, I realized that their lives apart from each other was a story worth telling, as well as unearthing the whole truth about why my mother vanished. That's how "The Magic In Life" originated, the third and final book about my family's saga. Perhaps in the future I'll write about my childhood and teenage years, growing up with my adoptive parents, but it'll be through a new book series.

Erasmus Cromwell-Smith II

Written at T.D.O.K., Summer of 2056

Acknowledgment

"Geniality" being a sequel was a challenge from the beginning. Well, in the end, more than twenty people collaborated in the crafting of this book. I will always be in debt to all of you for making Geniality, a book worthy of its predecessor, The Equilibrist.

To the ad hoc members of "Geniality" pseudo editor's committee, you are an eclectic and diverse group composed of published authors, historians, pedagogues, and intellectuals. Your feedback was invaluable. As important though, was all of you experiencing an intense emotional connection and reaction to the book. It was highly fulfilling and inspirational, making the continuation of a very intense and introspective journey, even more so. Thank you!

To my team: Amy, Alfredo, Andrea, Ana Julia (RIP), Barry, Bobby, Burt, Chabelin, Charles, Elisa, German, Janet, Jose, Maria Elena, Mark, MaryAnn (RIP) and Mitch. Without your hard work, "Geniality" would not have been possible.

Finally, it is only because of my family's faith and support that I was able to create this sequel independently and unconstrained of any commercial editing or vetting filters, which resulted in making Geniality a genuine and authentic creation. As with its predecessor, the Equilibrist, your support enabled me to release to the world, a craft that is exacting, word by word, to the way I intended and to the form I created it.

Thank you!

About the author:

Erasmus Cromwell-Smith II is an American writer, playwright and poet. The Happiness Triangle -part of The Equilibrist series- was crafted through a very intense and intimate introspective dive into the author's own life experience and wisdom. It is his first published work.